THE ONE PERCENT

TALES OF THE SUPER WEALTHY AND DEPRAVED

EDITOR-IN-CHIEF: Roger Nokes
MANAGING EDITOR: Jay Butkowski
CONTRIBUTING EDITOR: Albert Tucher
ASSOCIATE EDITOR: Paul J. Garth
ASSOCIATE EDITOR: R.D. Sullivan
ASSOCIATE EDITOR: Rob D. Smith
GUARDIAN ANGEL: Jonathan Elliott
COVER ART: Heather Garth

ON THE WEB: **www.rockandahardplacemag.com**
ON FACEBOOK: **@RHP_Press**
ON TWITTER: **@RHP_Press**
ON B'SKY: **@rhppress.bsky.social**
BY EMAIL: **editors@rockandahardplacemag.com**

Rock and a Hard Place Magazine and other works released through RHP Press are a labor of love, produced by a team of volunteer editors to showcase the best in dark fiction, crime, dystopian fiction, and noir. To learn how you can support the mission of **Rock and a Hard Place Press** through tax-deductible donations, or by subscribing to the RHP Patreon, please visit the website, and click **"Support RHP"** through the main menu.

THE ONE PERCENT: TALES OF THE SUPER WEALTHY AND DEPRAVED
Copyright © and ™ 2023

Editor-in-Chief: Roger Nokes
Additional Editorial Staff: Jay Butkowski, Paul J. Garth, Rob D. Smith, R.D. Sullivan, and Albert Tucher

With Stories by: Steven-Elliot Altman, Tom Andes, C.W. Blackwell, Meirav Devash, James D.F. Hannah, Curtis Ippolito, Jesse Lee, Sean Logan, Eddie McNamara, Lin Morris, Esther Mubawa, Andrew Rucker Jones, AD Schweiss, Thomas Trang, Scott Von Doviak, Tim P. Walker, and Sam Wiebe

Cover by Heather Garth
Book design by Roger Nokes and Jay Butkowski

ISBN: 979-8-9878765-1-0 (Paperback)
ISBN: 979-8-9878765-2-7 (eBook)
Library of Congress Control Number: 2023952131

10 9 8 7 6 5 4 3 2 1

Published by Rock and a Hard Place Press, an imprint of Rock and a Hard Place Press, LLC, Woodbridge, NJ.
rockandahardplacemag.com
amazon.com/~/e/B08WPQG5YV

Printed in the United States of America

DEDICATION

For Elon Musk's chauffer, Jeff Bezos's doorman, Mark Zuckerberg's MMA instructor and anyone else who has to put up with their bullshit to put food on the table.

ACKNOWLEDGEMENTS:

Creation is rarely a solo enterprise. Even when there's just one person credited, there's usually a community that's been built up around that creator, that supports them through thick and thin, that stokes the fires of imagination, and encourages them to engage in that next great creative act.

At **Rock and a Hard Place**, we are so fortunate to have built up a community of authors, artists, and readers, who *get* us. We hope you enjoy this latest issue as much as we've enjoyed pulling it all together.

A special thank you to our Patreon subscribers who continue to show up in so many ways to support the mission of RHP:

Dustin Walker
Mark Pelletier
Rob Smith
Jay Bechtol
Susan Kuchinskas
Todd Robins
Susan Jessen
Richard Risemberg
Ted Flanagan
Chris Rhatigan
Ryan Citron

Contents

Foreword: It's the same old song

Welcome to the new order. It's the same as the old order.

We work hard and *they* get rich. *We* follow the rules and *they* flout them.

Now it looks like tech bros on yachts and private spaceships to the moon. A hundred years ago it was oil barons and railroad tycoons. People profit from the destruction of the planet just as they did off slave labor. It's a child digging minerals to power your smartphone just as it was young women burning to death in a t-shirt factory.

The issue of absurd wealth concentrated in the blood-soaked hands of the few is as much a constant in our history as war and racism.

With *The One Percent: Tales of the Super Wealthy and Depraved*, we give you stories of those at the top. Though these stories are fictional and are individual accounts of people at the highest tiers of our economic system, we hope that collectively they point to a larger systemic problem, which is the fact that our economic system incentivizes cut-throat nastiness. Having a system that rewards people for hoarding wealth and taking advantage of others means individuals with fewer scruples are more likely to rise to the top and that those that may have some basic sense of ethics or human empathy quickly learn to abandon it in order to compete.

To say that this is a systemic problem is not to absolve the individuals who benefit from the system from their guilt and culpability. They take part in it, uphold it, and further it for their own sakes. They're the architects of the system, the maintainers of the status quo.

We hope this volume serves as some small form of accountability, as a way of saying that, though we are forced to live in this system for our own survival, we are not blind to it. This is our way of saying that although they have taken the majority of our waking hours, they have not taken our creativity or our humanity.

In this collection, you'll read stories of glorious comeuppance. As one of our authors writes, there are spiders that "eat other spiders," and you'll read about people out of their depths, blinded by the promise of easy cash and paying for it in the end. But there are others still, who just get away with it, who treat people like pieces on a gameboard, and never learn their lesson—because in the end, they still come out on top.

What we tried to do is find a mix of the unrepentant and the unfazed. But we never want to glorify those captains of industry who profit from the misery of others. This anthology is about showcasing the problems of immense, unchecked wealth. It's not our usual fare of people struggling to eke out survival, but it is still presented with the trademark RHP brand of social justice and basic fairness. In this anthology, we let our authors do bad things to bad people . . . and the results are entertaining as fuck.

So, take this volume and enjoy it. Laugh at some of the outrageousness. Cry over the inhumanity. And rage at the insane injustice of it all.

-The Rock and a Hard Place Editorial Team
Roger, Al, Jay, Paul, Morgan and Rob
December, 2023

1

"Now there was a new spider plucking the threads—the kind that eats other spiders."

The Block and the Chain

C.W. Blackwell

They meet at the Plumed Horse in Saratoga, a Michelin Star restaurant with tableside duck consommé and the kind of desserts that float by on elegant glass-domed carts. He's relieved when she walks through the door—in these days of deep fakes and filters, it's hard to know if a *TikTok ten* will translate to an *IRL ten*, and from what he can tell, everything checks out. He lets her wait at the hostess stand for a moment, watching as she scans the room. He doesn't want to seem eager. When he finally stands and waives her over, he adjusts the cuff of his sleeve so everyone can see the rose-gold Bulova on his wrist.

"Chaz?" she says, with cautious eyes.

He knows it's an act—based on her profile, there's nothing cautious about her.

"Cecilia? Please, sit. I ordered you a Malvasia Bianca."

She hangs her clutch on the chair and settles into the immaculate white-cloth two-top. She slowly drags a long strand of brown hair behind her ear and smiles broadly—it's enough to trigger her dimples. Chaz knows this must be a signature move, and he's surprised she's played it so early. Still, he gives her the reaction she's looking for and offers a smile in return.

He wants to reward her for acting pretty and insecure.

"Sorry I'm late," she says.

"It's only a minute or two."

His eyes drift over her dress.

"I didn't recognize the flag on your profile," he says.

"Panamá," she says. "I'm from Panamá City. You been there?" She plays up the long vowels in the word *city*. She thinks he has an accent kink, and she's not wrong. Chaz won't date a woman unless he knows English is her second language. He thinks it gives him an advantage—and power is an aphrodisiac.

"I've never been," he says. "But if you're any indication, I'll have to change that."

"That's very nice of you."

It's the most reassurance he'll give until dinner ends.

From now on, everything will be about him.

"It's called the blockchain," he says later, when the wine comes. He rolls a glass of Mourvèdre in the air and waits for her to admit she doesn't know what that is. "It's a digital ledger—a way to do business without gatekeepers like banks or federal governments. It's okay—not many people understand it. But that's how I make a living. It's like being involved with the Internet in '89, or computing in the 1940s. I'm one of the early adopters. There are exchanges for cryptocurrencies and I help clients navigate them. It's all very lucrative for me."

"Is it like Bitcoin?" she asks.

This time he doesn't reward her with a smile.

"That's one of many digital currencies, but you're on the right track."

"I should introduce you to my tío Inácio," she says. "He's always looking for new ways to move money around." But she covers her mouth after she says it, and her eyes track left and right to see if anyone is listening.

"Your uncle's a businessman?"

"Yes." She lowers her voice. "He lives in Panamá, but he visits the Bay Area all the time. He's in town this week for something called vulture capital."

"You mean *venture capital?*"

"Yes, that's it. I'll give him your number if it's okay with you."

Chaz worries the power dynamic has shifted now that she has something to offer beyond what's under her dress.

"I might have room for one more client," he says. "No guarantees, though."

❖

It bothers him that Cecilia doesn't fawn over his high-end loft on Santa Cruz Avenue. She's the first of his dates to see it after the remodel—the exposed brick and concrete countertops. The NFT nudes framed over the bed. He worries that she's seen better lofts in other parts of town. When he undresses her, he makes sure to toss her clothes all over the room so he can lay in bed and watch her search for them afterward. He sometimes wonders if this is another one of his kinks or just a personality disorder.

Later, when the rideshare comes, he walks her down to the lamp-lit street and they hug like friends and kiss on the cheek. They don't make plans to see each other again—that's another dance that must be carefully choreographed—but as he's riding the small elevator back to his loft, his phone rings and he assumes she's forgotten something.

He answers—it's a voice he doesn't recognize.

"I understand you are the crypto guy," says the voice, a hoarse, accented croak that triggers the hair on his forearms.

"I'm sorry, who am I speaking with?"

"My name is Inácio Narra. My niece sent me your number tonight, says you're the *real deal.*"

"Of course—*Cecilia,*" says Chaz. He clears his throat and turns his crypto-bro vibe up to maximum sleaze. "She spoke highly of you and your business. She said we should meet."

"Yes, I agree. Don't you? How about tonight?"

The phosphorescent hands of the Bulova read one in the morning.

"We must be in different time zones," says Chaz.

"I can assure you we are in the same time zone, amigo. Here's what I propose. Meet me at your office in thirty minutes to discuss opening a new account with your firm. My driver already has the address. For your trouble, we will only consider seven-digit wire transfers. Do we have a deal?"

Chaz enters the loft and fingers the blinds as if he might find Mr. Narra in a tinted sedan idling on the street, watching him.

"Yeah sure," says Chaz. He doesn't like to be summoned, but he also senses a tinge of urgency, and it excites something in his cells. "Let's do it."

◆

When Chaz reaches his boutique streetside office in Los Gatos, all the lights are on and there's a Mercedes idling at the curb. The door is unlocked. There's a sharp smell of cologne inside, something like tobacco and eucalyptus. A large man blocks the doorway of his personal office and Chaz knows this cannot be Mr. Narra. The vibe is wrong: he's too young and his eyes are dull and flat like someone is controlling him from a distance. The large man beckons Chaz forward and pats him down from pits to ankles.

"No need for that, Santos," says a voice—*Narra's voice*. It's coming from deeper in the office. "We are all professional businessmen here."

The large man steps aside, and Chaz sees Mr. Narra seated at his desk with his feet up. He's a petite man with a neatly trimmed beard that has turned mostly gray, save for a darker patch on his chin. Silver curls hang at his ears and forehead, black chevrons for eyebrows. He has the kind of lines on his face that make him both handsome and fearsome at the same time.

"If you're wondering how we got in," says Mr. Narra, "it would be easier to just skip that part and get straight to business."

Chaz considers his personal office a spider web for wealthy clients. A sticky trap for easy five-figure commissions. But now there was a new spider plucking the threads—*the kind that eats other spiders.*

"Normally my clients like to talk about the blockchain and all the emerging crypto currencies available to them," says Chaz. He squeezes into one of the chairs he reserves for his clients—too small by design—and folds his hands awkwardly in his lap. "It's an exciting opportunity, but it's also an evolving landscape and you should—"

"Can you tell me about chain-hopping?" says Narra. He leans forward and now his blue-gray eyes have a sinister interest that almost looks like hunger.

"Sure, I mean you just convert digital currencies through a series of different exchanges to achieve greater anonymity."

"Do you know of any rules against it?"

Chaz turns up his palms like he's about to fill the room with insight.

"In my business you learn there are two sets of rules, Mr. Narra. There is a set of rules for the regular nine-to-five chump who thinks it's a civic duty to let everyone shove taxes and bank fees and interest charges straight up his colon. And there are rules for smart men who routinely get *ten-X* on their investments through pure ingenuity and creative financial management. My guess is you are one of the latter, am I right? If so, I'm not so much concerned about the rules, and you shouldn't be either. We can usually work around them."

Mr. Narra nods approvingly.

Chaz knows it's the answer he was hoping for.

"In that case," says Mr. Narra. "I would like to open an account. How long would it take to chain-hop five million dollars?"

Chaz feels sweat trailing down the back of his neck. He hopes Mr. Narra doesn't notice, but with those eager, hungry eyes how could he not?

"We'll do a little paperwork and I'll send you the account numbers in the morning. You can begin the wire transfers whenever you'd like," says Chaz. "When the money lands, I'll make you my top priority. How does that sound?"

Mr. Narra signals to Santos, who unshoulders a black gym bag and sets it atop the desk. Chaz knows without unzipping it that it's full of dirty cash. He can see the hard corners pressing through the nylon. *It excites him.*

"I like to pay my commissions separately. I don't like when the account balances shrink without explanation, okay? It's six percent, but it's all cash—so you can do whatever you want with it. Live your best life. I've got more nieces to fuck if you're interested."

"I understand—yes. I can do that."

"Good. And one more thing, amigo. When I call you, I expect you to answer. No text, no voicemail. I don't care if you're in a meeting or at the dentist or getting the best blowjob of your life. You answer. Every fucking time—you answer. *Understand?*"

"Yes. I understand."

❖

The first sign of trouble comes on a rainy morning in November.

Chaz's phone goes *ding ding ding* as he turns the corner onto University Avenue, an umbrella in one hand and a 190-degree venti caramel Macchiato—*hold the foam and the tip*—in the other. He doesn't check the texts until his assistant, Kimberly, greets him at the door with a wild look and the sound of landlines at DEFCON ONE.

"Did you hear?" she says, with a TV remote in her hand.

He sets the umbrella behind the door, glances at the phone on her desk.

All the lights are blinking red.

"Hear what?"

She swings the remote at the TV, jerking the volume button as if it would somehow work faster that way. Chaz sees a pretty TV anchor with glossy lips and a robot stare. She's talking about one of the main crypto exchanges Chaz uses, and how the company that runs it has filed for bankruptcy. There's even a photograph of the company's CEO, a young tech bro named Zander Holman-Reid, with the caption: POSSIBLE INDICTMENT?

The anchor repeats the words *liquidity* and *loss* and *shockwaves*.

Chaz's cell phone rings in his hand.

It's Mr. Narra.

FUCK.

Chaz answers—at least he thinks he answers. The words stick to his tongue like bad medicine.

"Sounds like my crypto-wizard is having quite the day," says Narra. "Hopefully it doesn't mean I'm having one, too."

"I'm about to make some phone calls," says Chaz. "I'm sure it's not as bad as it sounds."

"You better be sure." Narra's mouth is close to the phone and Chaz can hear the topography of his throat as he speaks. The tiny balls of phlegm, the tobacco-scarred bronchial tubes. Maybe he's smoking a cigarette, maybe he's already smoked too many. "Because it sounds very bad to me. How much of my account has been anonymized?"

"About half."

"And how much of that is liquid?"

"Also half."

"Well that's not so good. You might have to go to extraordinary lengths to make me whole. I trust that I am still your top priority?"

Chaz has visions of his tongue slowly pulled through a slit in his throat to make a Colombian necktie. *Is Panama near Colombia?*

"Yes, of course you are my top priority."

"Good, amigo. That's very good."

The day feels like a week.

By the end of the week—*eons.*

Clients line up at his office to dress him down. They call him a fraud and a liar. He hears comparisons to Bernie Madoff. He doesn't really care about name-calling, but the legal threats worry him. Everything is beyond his control and he can't help any of it—it's like someone emptied a tube of crazy glue into the crypto market.

Amid the media circus and the unending drop-ins, Chaz breaks the one promise he swore to keep. It happens while a client named Van Hoevel is standing in his office, telling him about a bulldog lawyer who will *turn him inside out*. Chaz doesn't know what that means exactly, but during the litany of threats and oaths, he lets a call from Mr. Narra go unanswered.

When he sees the notification, a rotten feeling grows.

He waits until later that night, a bottle of twenty-year Macallan at the ready. He plays Narra's message, and the first time through, he's relieved—there's no yelling or swearing, nothing spoken at all. All he hears is the slow rasp of Narra's breath, like it's an old school answering machine and he's waiting for Chaz to pick up. The message breaks apart into white noise with each slow breath. It's like that for fifteen seconds—then there's the sparkwheel of a cigarette lighter, the crackle of tobacco, a long drag, and the message ends.

He replays it again and feels unsettled.

By the tenth time through—*he's terrified.*

He's drunk when he calls Cecilia.

She doesn't pick up, so he calls again.

And again.

When she finally answers, it sounds like she's at a party. A bass track thrums in the background like a heartbeat jacked on crank. She shouts into the phone—partly because of the loud music, partly because she's annoyed.

"It's about your uncle," he says.

"I already gave him your number." She says it fast like she's trying to end the call in a hurry.

"I know—we're doing business together. I just need to talk to you."

"What do you want, Chaz?" There's a bite to her voice, as if she's close to hanging up on him. "We went on like *one date* and I never heard from you again. Get to the point."

"I fucked up with him. I think he's really upset with me."

"That's your problem. Leave me out of it."

"I'm not asking for help, here. I just need to know something about him."

There's a long pause and the music fades. It sounds like she's gone into a private room or stepped outside.

"He's family," she says. "I won't tell you much."

"I just need to know how dangerous he is. Like if he's upset with me, you know, would he try to hurt me? What's his deal, really?"

"If you've angered him, you'll want to make it up to him very quickly."

"Yeah, but what if I can't? I mean, what if he thinks I really screwed him over—like a *million-dollar-plus* screw-over? I'm kind of freaking out here."

A long pause, then: "Goodbye, Chaz. Don't call me again."

"*No no—wait!*"

The call ends.

He tries texting her, but all the messages go unread.

◈

The news only gets worse.

Next day, he learns Zander Holman-Reid has fled to some Caribbean country with minimal extradition laws and a local court has issued an injunction against market-making on the exchange. It's a clumsy move—the courts don't know how to handle this. Panic begets more panic. The contagion spreads to other tech markets and there are worries it could bleed into the broader financial market. Trading is briefly halted on the NASDAQ.

There's a raw pain in Chaz's stomach like a fist clenching.

He does a line of cocaine off the concrete countertop and texts Kimberly, tells her not to come in for the rest of the week. She asks if she'll still get paid, and he says no. Kimberly quits. It doesn't hurt his feelings—he didn't hire her for her clerical skills.

More cocaine.

The fist unclenches, but the paranoia grows.

Some steampunk-looking Derringer pistol comes out of the drawer, and he paces around the loft, wagging it at the walls, shouting obscenities at the TV.

He orders GrubHub from an overpriced American-style bistro in Saratoga. He won't touch french fries unless they're double-fried with garlic aioli. When the order comes, he tells the delivery guy to leave it at the door, but the guy doesn't listen, just keeps knocking.

They always leave it at the door—*don't they?*

Knock knock knock.

Chaz checks the doorbell camera. Some skinny kid with an Adam's apple like the knuckle of a big toe. He's wearing earbuds and bobbing his head to a mid-tempo beat. Chaz has done so much cocaine he can almost feel the beat clapping in his veins.

KNOCK KNOCK KNOCK.

"Just fucking leave it," he shouts.

KNOCK KNOCK KNOCK.

Chaz throws open the door, tears the bag out of the kid's hands, and screams *fuck you* in Neanderthal. The kid sees the gun and his eyes clock wide. He pedals back, holds up his hands, and bolts down the hall.

The fries are cold, but Chaz eats them anyway.

❖

He's crying in the shower when they come for him.

Chaz sees them as he staggers out of the bathroom with a big white robe and bloodshot eyes. He freezes. They seem bored and disinterested, like they're waiting for a table at a restaurant. Like breaking into high-end lofts is part of their day-to-day.

"You look like a wet bag of cocaine," says Mr. Narra. He puffs on a cigarette and flicks the ashes onto the floor. Santos stands at his side, hands on his hips. His holstered pistol says *don't even fucking try.*

"I need more time," says Chaz.

A laugh—it sounds like a cat hissing.

"Time to do what? More drugs and alcohol?"

"I can get your money out."

"No, you can't. You don't think I've looked into this? Even if you could get the money out, the currency valuation has fallen through the floor. Beyond the floor, really—straight down into the devil's greasy asshole. Who knows if it will ever recover?"

"None of this is my fault. It just happened."

Mr. Narra doesn't like this.

"What a childish statement. *It just happened?*"

"Everyone's scrambling. Nobody knows what to do."

Mr. Narra gives a disgusted look and tilts his head to Santos, who unholsters a flat black pistol with a suppressor and levels it at Chaz.

"Adelante," says Santos, flicking the pistol at the door.

Chaz holds his hands up.

"Where are we going?"

Santos's eyes grow large and a growl burbles deep in his throat.

"Santos never repeats anything," says Mr. Narra. "If he does, it means your ass. I'd better move if I were you."

Chaz shuffles to the door, glancing around the loft to see where he left his Derringer. He doesn't see it anywhere. In the hallway, he considers making a run for it, but the halls are too long and Santos is too close. He feels the pistol in his spine, urging him onward toward the elevator. He thinks they're going down to the street, but they take the stairs instead—one flight up to the roof. Santos and Narra are now wearing black masks and leather gloves—*were they wearing them the whole time?*

"I want to tell you a funny story," says Mr. Narra, amid the woosh and whir of rooftop ventilation units. It's late evening and there's a spectacular Central Coast sunset playing out over the Santa Cruz Mountains, redwoods serrating a dark orange sky. To the east, evening commuters claw their way home along Highway 17 toward Santa Cruz, headlights winding through the gloom like a string of patio lights. "When I was a young man, I worked for my father. I kept an eye on things, made sure everyone did their jobs. Mid-management—but for the transshipment business. Mostly moving Colombian cocaine through the canal. I'm sure none of this surprises you. Most of the time, it was an easy job. But when someone betrayed our trust, there was this thing we'd do. I'd arrange for the Port Authority to take us out into the canal—we had plenty of PA guys in our pockets—and then we'd wrap the guy in a heavy steel chain and loop it through a few concrete cinder blocks and sink him in the canal. You have to make an example of somebody now and then to keep order, as I'm sure you can imagine." Here comes that sinister, feline laugh again. "So when I first heard the term *blockchain*, that's what I imagined. I can't untangle the two concepts. I must have sunk a dozen men in that canal. All tied up in blockchains—*cadenas de bloques*."

They're standing at the edge of the building. A three-foot-tall barrier encircles the rooftop, and Chaz sees a small step stool pressed against the rail. Beside the stepstool is a heavy steel chain coiled in a mound, and there's a concrete cinder block resting beside it.

Chaz knows he's going to die.

He makes one last attempt to flee—he spins around Santos and runs toward the stairwell door. Santos is quick—he brings the pistol down on Chaz's head and opens up a two-inch gash in his scalp. Chaz goes down, blood spilling over his white terrycloth robe. Santos stands him up again.

The world blurs.

"Please," says Chaz. He says it to the fuzzy masked figures before him. He says it to the universe. He knows that begging is his only play now. "I learned my lesson. I'll do better. I'll make it right."

"It isn't you who needs a lesson," says Mr. Narra. "You are beyond instruction. We considered killing you with that stupid cartoon gun we found in your apartment to make it look like a suicide. Thing is, it's my other financial partners who really need to learn from this. The financial landscape is evolving, as you recently told me. My people need to be reminded where they stand."

Chaz only hears half of it. The rest is drowned by the sound of chains coiling around his neck. Santos places the cinder block atop the ledge. The chain is wrapped through its hollow center to make a crude anchor.

"De rodillas," says Santos.

Chaz doesn't know what this means.

He blinks at the city lights. There are pigeons flying low over the cityscape, returning to their night roosts. The fang of a crescent moon rises out of the South Bay smog.

The cinder block vanishes.

In its place: the chain snakes wildly against the ledge.

It makes a sound like spare coins emptying from a glass jug.

The slack runs out and the chain snaps tight.

The world spins and wrenches apart.

"Everyone will be so excited to see you."

Most Likely to Succeed

Scott Von Doviak

You're a regular guy. Not like those other world-famous billionaires. Bezos, Musk, Zuckerberg—they're all aliens wearing human skin, they talk like ChatGPT is writing their dialogue. Not you. You drink Bud Light, not wine from your vineyard in Saint-Marcaire. Sure, you have a luxury box at AT&T Stadium, but that's just for business. You always sneak away during the game and spend at least one quarter in the stands, whooping it up with the true Cowboys fans. Unimaginable wealth hasn't changed you. That's why you're going to your twentieth high school reunion.

You wish it could have been a surprise. The looks on the old gang's faces when you strolled into the gym at old William Polk Hardeman Memorial High School—that would have been priceless. Unfortunately, that wasn't possible. You're bringing the film crew from your new reality show with you, and they had to get releases and NDAs signed by everyone in advance. Still, it's going to be a blast. Everyone will be so excited to see you.

You haven't kept in touch with many of your old classmates recently, but you're sure you'll be able to pick up right where you left off. You all came from the same humble beginnings in Purgatory Springs, Texas. Like most of your old friends, you're the son of an oilman. True, your father owned the company and their fathers worked for him, but you never got any special treatment because of that. You made the football team on your own merit. Who else would have been QB1? It certainly wasn't your fault the team went 3-7 your senior year. A quarterback is only as good as his receivers and running backs. No one ever blamed you for the first season in twelve years Hardeman High didn't make the playoffs.

In the back of the Escalade limo on the way to Purgatory Springs, you flip through your old yearbook. It all comes flooding back. Briles. Timmons. McFadden. Hightower. Friends for life. Jessica Norton. Holy shit. How many times did you jerk off to this picture of her in her cheerleader uniform? You could do it right now. Just raise the partition between you and the driver. What did Matthew McConaughey say in *Dazed and Confused*? I get older, they stay the same age. But no. She'll be there. If she's still hot, you'll invite her back to the hotel. No way she'll say no.

Hardeman High comes into view, right where you left it, between the Gilman Fertilizer plant and the nursing home. The new high school opened last year across town, and Hardeman was scheduled for demolition in the fall as the town planned to sell the land for new development. You swooped in and bought the parcel just to save Hardeman for a few more months. Just for this night. Your classmates would be so grateful if they knew, but they never will because you bought the land through a shell game of offshore companies that will never be linked to you. You'll sell it at a profit soon enough, but having the reunion in the old gym will make it even more special, and since it's not a school anymore, the organizers can serve booze. You're covering the open bar, too. That's not a secret. Anything for your old friends.

The Escalade pulls up in front, the camera truck right behind. Once the crew is in position and ready to roll, you push open the gym door and head inside.

Nelly's "Hot in Herre" blasts from the sound system. Disco lights flash as your former classmates get down on the dance floor. There's a line at the bar, but no matter. Someone is already pressing a drink into your hand.

"Holy shit, Trevor Longwood," says the grinning man, bumping his glass against whatever he just handed you. "I heard you were coming, but I didn't believe it."

You sneak a glance to make sure the cameras are capturing this genuine interaction, even as you're desperately trying to remember who this is.

"You don't know me. I'm here with my wife," he says, saving your bacon. "I'm Don Quigley."

"Cool. And your wife is?"

"Jessica Quigley. Well, you knew her as Jessica Norton."

Well, shit. That's going to make it a little harder to sneak her back to your hotel, but not impossible. Still, you need to get a look at her first and make sure it's worth the effort. Her husband is no prize, that's for sure.

"Of course," you say. "Where is Jessica?"

"Oh, she's out there dancing. Never really been my thing. I'm a country music fan, never cared for this—" He seems to notice the cameras for the first time. "Well, not much of a dancer, that's all. But shit, I can't believe I'm talking to Trevor fucking Longwood! You know, lotta folks out here think you're killing the oil and gas industry with your fusion batteries, but they just gotta get with the times. I bought ten shares in Nukleus just last week."

"Well, you did the smart thing, Don. Let's get rich together, what do you say?"

"Hell yeah!"

"The Avenging American" by Toby Keith kicks in on the sound system and Don hollers and pumps his fist.

"Now that's what I'm talkin' about! We'll put a boot up your ass!"

"All right, Don! I'm gonna say hi to some of my old friends."

You motion the camera crew on. You spot them near the bar: Timmons, Briles, Hightower. Your brothers from other mothers. You sneak up on Briles, wrap your arm around his neck, and run your knuckles over his bald head.

"Hot damn," he says. "The golden boy's here."

"Sheeyit, boy, I hope you didn't drive here in one of your Nukes," says Hightower. "Ain't nowhere to charge one of the sumbitches within three hundred miles of here."

"Doesn't matter," you say, winking at the camera. "Coast to coast on a single charge. Besides, you'll have 'em here soon enough."

"How's that?" says Timmons, shaking up his Miller Lite and spraying it in your face. You do a pretty good job of pretending you expected this and love it.

"I'm donating a hundred Nukleus 6Gs to the school district, sheriff's department, local businesses with more than ten employees. A dozen chargers, too. Once they're here, won't nobody be wanting to pay four bucks a gallon for gas. Charge it once a month, you're good to go."

"Tell you what," says Briles. "You'll pry my F-150 from my cold, dead hands."

"Well, let's hope it doesn't come to that." You laugh like you're joking. "Hey, where the fuck is McFadden?"

There's a notable shift in the energy. They know something you don't.

"He, uh, he didn't make it," says Hightower.

"That's too bad," you say. "Where's he living now?"

"He's not," says Briles. "Meaning he's not living now. He offed himself back in February."

"Holy fuck," you say. "I didn't know anything about that. What happened?"

"Well, he was working for your father at Longwood Oil and Gas. You must have known that."

"Sure, but Daddy passed back in 2012. That's when I cashed in my shares. What happened to the company after that, I didn't care to know."

That's not true, of course, but the truth isn't for the cameras. The truth is that your Uncle Reavis took over the company. Got big into fracking. You thought he was sullying the good family name. It was never proven that leakage from his toxic waste injection wells had poisoned the groundwater in Pecos Valley, but you know it's true. You decided to ruin Uncle Reavis. You lured him into a bid-rigging partnership with another oil company whose CEO was deep in debt to you. You helped that CEO flee to a country with no extradition on condition that he leave a full confession and trail of evidence behind. The day after Uncle Reavis was indicted, he drove his Porsche off the Pecos River High Bridge.

"The company went under," says Hightower, telling you something you pretend you don't already know. "Suddenly McFadden's shares were worthless and he was out of a job and over half a million in debt. He wanted to make sure his wife and kids didn't end up with nothing, and he had an insurance policy, so one Saturday he went hiking in Big Bend and had an 'accidental' fall."

"Maybe it really was an accident." Hell, you never know. And even if it wasn't, you can't blame yourself. McFadden's debts were his own problem. A responsible family man would never owe a cent to any man, company, or government.

"Sure," says Hightower. "Anyway, we've got a little tribute planned for him in a bit."

"Good. Hey listen, y'all, I gotta have a word with my producer for a minute. You know, TV stuff. Y'all signed those releases, right? I'm gonna make y'all famous."

You slap backs and head off with Morgan, the producer of *The Longwood Chronicles*.

"You got all that about my old friend McFadden, right?"

"Absolutely, boss. Solid gold."

"Yeah. We can cut in some teary-eyed shots of me, right?"

"For sure. We'll do a confessional where you talk about how hard it was for you to hear that, how much he meant to you, all that shit."

"Yeah, yeah, and look, I need you to find out about the widow, the kids. I'm gonna make a big anonymous donation to them. Who do you think we can leak that to?"

"That reporter from *Forbes* is still working on the cover story about you. We can get it to him."

"Perfect. All right. Now listen, I'm gonna need a little discretion in a bit. An old crush is here and, well, her husband's with her. Maybe you can pull him aside, do a one-on-one? We'll never use it, but just to get him out of the room, you know?"

"Absolutely. Just point him out and we'll take care of it."

Once the crew has Don Quigley sequestered, you zero in on Jessica. You're not disappointed. She's in great shape. If she's had a little work done, it's subtle. Best of all, she seems very happy to see you.

"So what are you up to these days?" you ask.

"I guess you don't get back this way much. I'm a reporter at KPFA, Channel 5."

"No shit? Wow, that's fantastic."

"I would have loved to bring my own camera crew here tonight, but the NDAs your people made us sign. . ."

You shrug it off. "The lawyers handle all that. I really don't know anything about it."

"So you wouldn't mind doing a sit-down with me later?"

"To be absolutely honest, I was thinking we could do a little lie-down later. If you get my drift."

"Weird. I thought you met my husband."

"Come on, Jessica. That guy? You can do so much better."

"Oh, I remember your line. They don't call you Longwood for nothing."

"Ha, yeah. Only one way to find out for sure."

"Trevor, honey, I was best friends with Kasey Prince. I already know it's not true."

Your ears are burning, but your grin widens. You're not gonna let on how pissed you are. "Even if it wasn't true then, it is now."

"Oh. I see. Is this an exclusive?"

"It's off the record. Like everything else tonight. You want an exclusive one-on-one with me, it's gonna be back at my hotel room."

"Yeah? Are you prepared to answer questions about the studies on the fusion battery you've paid to suppress? Or do you need to keep those secret a few more days until the sale of Nukleus goes through? Oh, whoops—I'm not supposed to know about that, am I?"

Your grin widens. More teeth. You're Tom Cruise-ing this shit. "I don't know what you're talking about."

Because surely she doesn't know that production of your car battery requires nearly five times as much lithium as your closest competitor, or that the strip mines you've financed to claw the necessary rare metals out of the earth have already caused more environmental havoc than your Uncle Reavis ever dreamed possible. She can't possibly know about the secret test track at your Hudspeth County facility that has become a graveyard for the burnt-out husks of your new G6 model cars. As for the sale of the company, those rumors are always floating around. They just happen to be true this time.

Hightower gets you out of it. The house lights come up and he's on the stage at the far end of the gym, his face projected on the widescreen behind him.

"Class of 2003, whazzupppp?" He pumps his fist and the crowd goes wild, including you. "Hey, thanks, y'all, for coming out tonight. It's so great to see so many familiar faces. A lot of y'all were right here in this gym the night I fractured my forearm trying to block a pass by that giant dude from Fort Worth who won a championship with the Spurs a few years later."

A mix of laughter and cheers.

"Hey, listen, as your still-reigning senior class president, I've got a little treat for you. As y'all know, we lost our good friend and class treasurer Mitch McFadden earlier this year. Yeah, moment of silence, please."

You bow your head and dart your eyes. Morgan and the camera crew are back to capture the moment. Hightower lifts his head.

"All right, so Becca, Mitch's widow, found something while she was cleaning out the old house. I think some of y'all will remember it. Let's take a look."

The lights dim and a title card reading SENIOR NIGHT appears on the screen accompanied by the opening notes of a song you immediately recognize: "Good Riddance" by Green Day. You know what you're looking at. It's a video put together by McFadden featuring scenes from your graduation party in this very room. You had a copy of it once, years ago, but God knows whatever happened to it. Still, you watched it enough times back then that you still have it memorized. It's all the obvious choices, from the music on down. The cheerleaders doing a synchronized dance routine. The jocks laughing it up, high-fiving, dumping the contents of a flask into the punchbowl. Mark Hilburn running through the gym in a glittery Speedo, giving high fives along the way. And your personal favorite, the food fight you started by flinging a slice of pizza at Hightower's head.

Everyone at the reunion is laughing and having a good time. You know this will be a great humanizing moment for the show, and you're trying to play along, but you're still steamed over what Jessica just dumped on you. What she said is true. The studies will prove what you've known all along. The fusion battery is not all you've claimed it is. But that's just marketing. People hear 'fusion,' they think this is the next great leap forward in clean energy. And it is! But it's not *actual* nuclear fusion, and technically you've never said it was. Except when you got in that tweet war with a CalTech professor, but you deleted those pretty quickly. Your people have done a good job scrubbing them from the internet, casting doubt on the screenshots still being passed around.

But what the fuck? Are you supposed to sell your stockholders on "this is a slightly better electric car than the Tesla"? Nothing wrong with a little showmanship. Coast to coast on a single charge—that's strong branding. And it hasn't been proven untrue. Until now.

Your train of thought is derailed when the music abruptly cuts out. The slickly-edited video is replaced by shaky, out-of-focus footage of a camera tracking down a hallway. When the camera stops moving and the image becomes clear, you see two figures sitting on a bench in a locker room. One is passed out, slumped against the other, who takes a sip from a bottle of Lone Star and giggles. The former is Timmons. The latter is you.

More laughter comes from out of sight, from the person holding the camera. From McFadden.

"What happened to Timmons?" he says.

"Dude, fuckin' Jager shots happened to him. You got a Sharpie on you?"

"You gonna draw dicks on his face?"

A few uneasy laughs from your ex-classmates in the gym. You're not laughing.

"That's the idea. Why? You want to do something else to him?"

"I don't want to do anything to him. Is he breathing?"

"Hell yes, he's breathing. Ain'tcha, Timmons?"

Your younger self grabs Timmons by the hair and makes him nod. "See? He's fine."

"I dunno, man. Maybe we should get him some help."

"Christ, McFadden, you are such a pussy."

Here and now, you grab your producer and whisper in his ear. "Get someone to cut the power to this shit."

"Let's make this a night he'll never want to remember," the younger, dumber, drunker you says on screen. "Let's make it so he walks funny for a week and can't remember why."

And you know what comes next. You and McFadden never talked about it afterward, and you chased it from your memory as best you could. You told yourself it wasn't that bad. You didn't fuck him in the ass, for chrissakes. It was just a beer bottle. Just enough to leave a little puddle of blood in his tighty-whities and Timmons with a lot of questions. Questions you always meant to answer, but well, time slips away.

Nobody in the gym sees it happen. Just after you drain the bottle and wiggle it for the camera, the screen goes dark. Whether your producer got to the equipment or someone else decided everyone had seen enough, you don't know.

The lights come up, all eyes on you. Timmons takes the stage holding a microphone.

"There he is, ladies and gentlemen," he says, gesturing toward you. "Most Likely to Succeed, Trevor Longwood. Born on third base, thinks he hit a bases-clearing triple to win the World Series. I never knew what really happened until Becca McFadden found that footage on one of the tapes her husband shot on senior night. I don't know which was the most hilarious part: drunk-driving myself to the emergency room or having to take an AIDS test just in case."

He has more to say, but you don't hear it. The TV crew has closed ranks around you and hustled you the hell out of Hardeman High. Morgan meets you in the parking lot, holding a tape.

"I've got it," he says.

"So what? Everyone in there saw it."

"They all signed NDAs. Besides, what did they really see? Far as I know, you were only joking. Locker room talk, literally."

"Timmons knows. He might have copies of the tape. Could have digitized it."

"I'm sure he just wants money. Pay him off and the lawyers will keep it quiet."

You get in the back of the limo alone and roll up the partition. Morgan is probably right. You'll get out of this one the same way you always do. With a whole lot of money, you'll never even miss. But do you really want to take the chance? Especially when you have a foolproof Plan B?

There was always a possibility tonight would go sideways. Too many jealous people, all out to get you. And the ones who've known you the longest, they're the most jealous of all. Getting them all together in one place at the same time—a place of your choosing, even if they didn't know it—that was the stroke of genius.

Because you didn't just buy the high school. You also bought the fertilizer plant next door. The one that closed five years ago. The one that was last inspected in 2005. The one still stocked with tons of ammonium nitrate. Really, it's a miracle the place is still standing. It wouldn't take much more than a spark to set the whole thing off. And if someone happened to plant an incendiary device inside, it would be obliterated by the blast. No evidence would ever be found.

You hit a button on your phone. "Do it," you say.

The plant and the high school are more than five miles behind you now, but the explosion still fills the back window. The SUV rocks, but the driver keeps going. You'll see the crater on the morning news. The plant and the high school both vaporized. Sadly, the nursing home doesn't escape unscathed. They'll find eleven residents dead in the collapsed south wing. Not that they had much longer anyway.

You'll write some checks. They'll build a new nursing home and put your name on it. Hell, by the time you're done, they'll put your name on the new school, too.

Your phone is ringing. Your notifications are lighting up. You check Instagram. Someone posted the video two minutes ago, right before the explosion. Violated their NDA.

It's okay. The lawyers will squash it, scrub it. Morgan's right. What does it really prove anyway?

You watch the flames lick the sky, watch the poison clouds blot out your view of this dying planet only the ultra-rich will survive. In a year you'll cut the ribbon on the memorial to the class of 2003. Friends for life. You miss them already.

"She saw his white man's potbelly, his ponytail, the khaki shorts and shirt; they were all signs of wealth and smug comfort that she would never know."

Doris the Sculptor

Esther Mubawa

Doris Dimba was in the shade of an acacia tree, polishing a small sculpture of a hwange, a Zimbabwe fish eagle. An etching of the majestic bird was prominently displayed on the country's worthless bond notes.

When a green Land Rover came to an abrupt stop near her, sending up a cloud of grey dust from the shoulder of the road, she set down the oily rag she'd been using to polish the sculpture and took a scrap of cloth from her backpack and covered her nose and mouth with it and held it there until the dust had passed over her, but some of the dust, as always, settled in her hair. She'd have to wash it out when she returned home, using what little water she had managed to collect from her village's community well that morning.

A white man and woman got out of the Land Rover and went over to the sculptures Doris had placed on a series of rocks that were in the splintering shade of a single mopane tree. The white man and woman began to walk along the line of her sculptures. Both of them were wearing the khaki shirts and shorts and sun hats that seemed to Doris to be a kind of uniform white tourists wore when they went on a safari.

The woman, whom Doris judged to be in her fifties, had a slender, athletic shape to her; she now and then squatted down to look more closely at the sculptures through her sunglasses, ones of giraffes, lions, elephants, hippos, hwanges, and those of Shona women carrying buckets of water on their heads, a piece that was a favorite with white tourists. They often passed by the traditional Shona sculptures of men and women embracing or of a woman cradling a child.

Doris, hoping to make a sale, wrapped up the hwange in the oily cloth and made her way over to the man and woman.

The man, who was older than the woman, had a potbelly and a grey ponytail tied up with a strand of leather. He was also wearing sunglasses, preventing Doris from seeing his eyes. Maybe it was white culture, Doris thought, for white people to wear sunglasses. She wasn't sure. They often did.

"We like your work," the man said. He hadn't bothered to look in her direction.

"You have some beautiful pieces," the woman said.

"Thank you," Doris said. "I do my best."

"The Shona are master sculptors," the woman said. "I like the black serpentine stone they use. It's very lustrous."

"It's a form of sandstone only found in Zimbabwe, you know that's in an arc from the west of the country to the east, where we are now," the man said.

"You've told me before," the woman said.
"Have I?"

"Yes."

Doris had started to learn sculpturing from her grandfather when she was twelve. He had long since passed. When Doris thought of him, she saw his rough but gentle fingers that held a stone. The skill that he had taught her had helped her to survive for several years now. She was thirty-seven, had four children, and lived in the village of Muneni. It held only a cluster of brick homes and was in a valley down a steep embankment from where she displayed her sculptures on the side of the road, just past the Prince of Wales Overlook. From where Doris was, the road climbed up into the mountains to the Leopard Rock Inn on the border with Mozambique. That's where most tourists went. The nights in the mountains there were cool and the days warm. Doris had heard that Queen Elizabeth had stayed in the inn once, back before the Bush War, when Rhodesian colonial rule had come to an end in 1980 and President Mugabe had changed the county's name to Zimbabwe. But that was long before her time. She'd heard from elders in her village that life had been better for them under colonial rule, and she had no reason to disagree with them, but no one dared to say such a thing and risk having someone from ZANU-PF, the ruling party, pay them a visit in the middle of the night. She'd heard of people who had talked politics and never been seen again.

"Eran," the woman said, "isn't that a cute one?" The woman was pointing at a small piece Doris had made of an elephant.

"I'm no damn Republican," the man growled.

The woman laughed.

"What's so funny?" the man asked.

"You," the woman said.

"Buy it," she said, "and give it to Robert."

"That asshole. You don't know who a person is until they vote Republican."

"Don't start up again," the woman said. "We're on holiday."

"You're the one who mentioned Robert," the man said.

The woman looked at Doris and smiled.

The man and woman continued, walking along the line of sculptures. Then the man stopped before one of a giraffe. "How much is this one?" he asked.

"Seven dollars," Doris answered. She knew she had asked too much and looked down at her sandals. They needed to be stitched up along the seams once again.

The man grunted.

"Not much of a souvenir, a giraffe," the woman said.

"What makes you think I was planning on putting it in our living room, honey? I'll give it to Robert. It'll play into his racist ideas of what Africa is, black people dancing in grass skirts and wild animals."

Doris had often heard white people call each other honey. She could make no sense of it. Shona men, they just came right out and said, "I love you," not meaning it, only saying it to get what they wanted out of a woman, and too often the women fell for the line and within a few months were pregnant.

"Give me six," Doris said.

The couple continued to walk along past the display of sculptures. Doris hadn't sold a piece in more than three days and needed a few dollars to buy a sack of maize meal for her to make sadza.

She followed the couple as they walked along. The man and woman were mumbling to each other. Doris was certain that they were talking about her sculptures and were intentionally speaking in a way so that she could not understand what they were saying. Then the woman turned and, to Doris's surprise, asked, "Are you married?"

"I have four children," Doris answered, "two boys and two girls. The oldest girl is doing her "A" levels."

"You must be very proud," the woman said.

"But the school fees are so high, and they're in dollars now. Everyone wants dollars."

"Are you married?" the man asked.

"My husband is in South Africa working as plumber," Doris said, making up a story about him. "There's no jobs here. We're struggling."

"Half the country is down south," the man said. "Your husband sends you money?"

"From time to time," Doris said.

The truth was that Doris's husband had left to work in Durban several years before. They had kept in touch on WhatsApp when she could afford data, but she hadn't heard from him in more than a year now, and she was certain that he had found another woman and had no interest in returning to a two-room home that had neither plumbing nor electricity. He'd stopped sending money home. A year before, Doris had taken up with a man who lived in another village, hoping he'd help her out with school fees. He had a business drilling boreholes for drinking water and drove a Toyota Hilux, but all she'd gotten from him were a few meals and visiting a hotel in the nearby town of Mutare that had a bed with clean sheets.

"Look at that one, Eran," the woman said. She was pointing at the piece of a Shona woman balancing a bucket on her head. When Doris saw the piece, she always thought of herself. It saddened her to look at it. She, too, had to carry a plastic bucket of water on her head from the community well to her home, or she had to go to the river a few kilometers away with her family's laundry in the bucket on her head to do the laundry beside a bridge where lorries sped past and the dust that followed settled in the women's hair. The drivers always stopped to shout down to the women, "How about taking a ride with me?" Some of the younger women, after a few months of doing laundry, did just that, never to return to village life.

"How much?" Eran asked.

"Seven dollars," Doris said.

The man grunted again.

"Six," Doris said. Six would buy her a ten kg sack of maize meal that would last her and her children perhaps two weeks if she measured it out carefully. She had some eggs from layers that pecked around her house, and there was always blackjack, a wild vegetable, that grew along the banks of a nearby ditch that she could mix in with the eggs and fry up in oil. When she could afford a small jar of peanut butter, she added a spoonful of that. Her children were always thrilled when they had, along with the sadza, some peanut butter.

"Four dollars," the man said. He had taken up the piece and was holding it. He seemed to be admiring it, but it was difficult for Doris to read the minds of white people who wore sunglasses. They often picked up her sculptures, held them, smiled, and then placed them back on their stands before returning to their Land Rovers and driving off.

"Five," Doris said.

The man stared at her. He was about to put the sculpture back on the flat-rock stand it had been resting on when Doris said, "Okay, boss, four. But we are struggling."

"Aren't we all," he said. "Clean it up for us. It's dusty."

He handed the piece to Doris, and she and the man and the woman went over to the shade of the acacia tree, where she had been polishing the hwange. She picked up the oily cloth and cleaned off the dust from the sculpture and, as she was doing so, the man tossed into the grey dust beside her a five dollar bill.

"You have change?" he said.

"Sir," she said. "I only have bond notes."

"I can't exchange those at the airport."

"You could take them home as a souvenir, honey," the woman said.

"Find someone who has change," the man said.

"I'll have to walk all the way down to my village," Doris said. She pointed to the collection of red and grey brick homes of Muneni in the valley below the highway. Even from this distance, she could see her two sons playing with a car an uncle of theirs had made for them from baling wire and bottle caps. They pushed the cars along in the dirt of the street, using sticks.

The man said, "Are you going to get me my dollar? We have reservations at the Leopard Inn."

"Maybe you could just pay her five, honey."

"We agreed on four," he said.

Doris looked up into the white man's sunglasses, seeing her distorted face reflected in the lenses. Because of the grey dust that had settled into her, she thought she looked like the old woman in her village whose three husbands had died mysteriously. Now she was living in a home made of red bricks. In her garden, there was an avocado and banana tree and a maize field. The villagers thought she was a witch who had cast spirits on her husbands. That's why they had died. She had done all right for herself.

Doris looked at the five dollar bill lying at her feet, then at the woman, who was smiling sympathetically.

"I can give you bond notes, boss," Doris said. "We are struggling. I have my daughter's school fees to pay."

"We agreed on four," the man replied.

Doris picked up a hammer that was lying on the ground beside her.

"No!" the woman shouted. "No! Honey, only a dollar."

"We agreed on four," the man said. "Four it is."

Doris laid the sculpture of the woman on the flat rock that she used to steady the stones to make her sculptures before looking back up at the man again. She saw his white man's potbelly, his ponytail, the khaki shorts, and his shirt; they were all signs of wealth and smug comfort that she would never know.

Doris drew back the hammer.

"No!" the white woman screamed. "Please!"

Doris slammed the hammer down on the sculpture. Pieces scattered in the grey dust.

The woman shrieked.

"Arrogant woman," the man said, "I wanted to help you."

"It was only a dollar," the white woman said.

"These people," the man said.

"We better go," the woman said. "We don't want to be late for our fucking reservations."

"You were the one who picked the place out, and just because the damn Queen stayed there."

"How did I ever end up with you?"

"We were both drunk," the man said.

"But now I've sobered up."

The man reached down and picked up the five-dollar bill. "Some experience this vacation has been," he said.

"You got that right. Quite the fucking experience."

"Shut up."

The two walked off to the Land Rover.

Doris took the hwange and continued where she'd left off, polishing it with that oily cloth, now and then looking over the edge of the cliff at her sons playing with their cars in the dirt.

4

"'Preacher, I pray to God every night, but I put my trust in a Glock 19.'"

Haggling Over Price

James D.F. Hannah

Wanna hear a joke?

A preacher wakes up on the most beautiful Sunday morning ever, and he can't bear to think about having to spend it in church, so he calls up his assistant, says he don't feel well, packs up his golf clubs and drives to a course in another town where no one knows him. He tees off on the first hole, and a big gust of wind catches the ball and carries it an extra hundred yards and drops it right in the hole for a hole-in-one. An angel's watching all this, and he says to God, "What'd you do that for?" God smiles and says, "Who's he gonna tell?"

Not funny?

Telling jokes wasn't never my strong suit, I suppose. When I was behind the pulpit, I'd throw one or two in, every sermon. My daughter called 'em "groaners," 'cause that's the sound you heard from the congregation. Or she called 'em "dad jokes." But if you're a dad and you're telling the joke, that makes all of 'em dad jokes anyway, right?

Okay, here's one I couldn't never tell when I was preaching: Guy walks up to this lady and asks her, "Would you sleep with me for a million dollars?" She eyes him up and says, "Sure." Then he says, "Would you sleep me for fifty bucks?" You can tell that ticks her off 'cause she says, "What kind of woman do you think I am?" The guy leans toward her and says, "We've done established that. Now we're haggling over price."

Still not funny? Fair enough. After all, you're probably more wondering what I'm doing here in your house, the middle of the night, holding a gun to your head. How I got past your security and your big-time team of bodyguards.

That don't matter right now. Irksome, I bet, for a man like you, always got someone on salary, ready to pull your tail out of the fire. But we both know they're only loyal as long as the money keeps flowing.

No, it's the other ones who are your true loyalists. You got a country full of believers to shame a fancy mega church. Every one of 'em worshipping what it is you're selling.

When I was preaching, best I had was fifty or sixty on Sunday morning. Back in Cole Creek, Kentucky.

I hadn't figured you'd heard of it. Most no one has. No reason to.

When I started out, it was just Carrie Ann and me. High school sweethearts. Got married right after graduation. It took us a few years and a bunch of tries to get pregnant before we had our little girl. Our Danielle.

Yes, we did name her after Daniel in the Bible. Not everyone catches that. Good on you, listening on Sunday mornings.

"God is my judge." That's what the name Daniel means. Carrie Ann wanted that. Felt it was important.

God is my judge.

Now I should tell you, I was a big supporter of yours. Well, your organization. You don't grow up where I did and not have a gun or three in the house. My old man, he had his rifles and shotguns on a big ol' rack right above the console TV, bullets and shells there on shelves next to the Avon bottles my momma used to decorate with. And we didn't touch those guns 'cause we knew if we did, my daddy would take the hide off of us.

It was a different time. Back then, your group said you were about sportsmanship and hunting. You had ads in the scout magazine with bull's eyes on them and if we took and shot up that ad with a BB gun and did good enough, you'd send a marksmanship certificate. My momma framed mine. She and my daddy were right proud of that.

I'm telling you this so you understand I'm not one of those people. The ones carrying signs, calling guns evil. Folks who've never held a pistol in their hands or know what it's like to pull the trigger. Who don't get how satisfying it can be to go into the woods on a Saturday morning and set a deer into your sights and to do it right. Respectfully. Even popping off a few rounds on old bottles and cans. There's something right pleasing about it. Enjoyable.

I raised Danielle 'round guns. We had 'em in the house. I did treat it different than my dad, keeping my pistol in a locked box under the bed, and all the rifles in a cabinet.

I can't remember when I realized y'all weren't out there talking about hunting anymore. Now it was how everyone needed to have a gun, no matter what. Next thing I knew, I'm at the grocery store and my next-door neighbor has a pistol hanging off his belt. Sometimes there'd be a guy with a rifle strapped across their back. And they're talking to you normal-like, asking how the high school football team's looking this season, or who's directing the Christmas play?

The folks at my church, whew, they were all in on what you were sellin'. Talking about how owning a gun was a God-given right, like it was something that came down off the mountain with Moses, an eleventh one scratched there in the margins. They bought guns like they were food, until their houses were full and there was a couple in every room. Taking photos with 'em, putting 'em on tops of Bibles, sending family pictures at Christmas, them and their rifles and pistols on Facebook.

I asked my head deacon about it. Mike'd always been a level-headed guy, but he'd taken a turn down this road in recent years, had himself an arsenal. He told me, "Preacher, I pray to God every night, but I put my trust in a Glock 19."

What do you even say to that?

I bet you love hearing this, right? 'Cause it's your job. To make people think they have to have a gun. That they can't have enough guns. Telling how the government wants to take their guns and if they take their guns, they're taking their freedom, too. That somehow the gun, it's more important than anything else. What's the thing y'all like to say? Oh yeah, how the Second Amendment is the one that protects all the others.

Like if the government was bound and determined to get your guns, they couldn't get 'em. Son, they got drones controlled by this kid with a joystick in Colorado. He could fly one of those things straight up your ass, you'd never know it was there until you farted and heard the boom, and you got people acting like they're gonna go "Red Dawn" on the military.

You've sold them more than guns, my friend; you've sold a bill of goods they can't collect.

It might be ignorance on my part, or I was keeping my head stuck in the ground, I don't know, but I didn't pay much mind. Even as my friends got more and more scared about things that didn't exist, boogeymen they thought were coming for them or their children. Things they read on the internet or heard on AM radio. Even when the economy went belly-up and people had to leave hollers where they'd grown up, and go somewhere they'd never been just so they could work.

There were the ones who couldn't do it, couldn't leave, and they used their guns on themselves and their families, because they couldn't bear the thought of moving away from the mountains, outside of walls they'd known their whole lives.

Danielle decided to go off to college. Said she felt she was being called to be a teacher. I wasn't so sure, but I also couldn't tell her to not listen to her heart. I guess I hoped she'd come back to the creek and teach there once she was done.

But she didn't. That's not how God works. She went to the city and got a job teaching second grade. She'd call her mother and me every week and tell us about it. She loved those little ones. Talk about how funny and sweet they were. How she saw so much of the future when she looked in their eyes.

Some nights, though, I couldn't sleep for worrying. What if something happened like on the news. Didn't seem like anywhere was safe. Knowing all it takes is one person buying one of those guns—the ones designed to do nothing more than kill other people—and they walk in somewhere and pull the trigger, and it changes lives. Out of nowhere you've got people burdened with a grief that's almost too heavy to carry.

After anything like that happens, the politicians show up and start in. They got the idea now of, oh, let's give the teachers guns. Danielle laughed at that one. "They don't trust us with what books to teach kids, and they expect us to carry guns in class?"

I'll bet you saw dollar signs every time one of those shootings happened. I know, I know, you don't make the guns or sell the guns, but you sure as fire make money from 'em. Your organization is the one telling people they need guns. You're the ones giving money to all these Congressmen and legislators so they can tell people how much God wants them to have as many guns as they want and to take 'em with 'em everywhere. You got some gun companies paying you a percentage for every gun they sell.

Don't try to tell me you're nothing but a messenger. You're making millions selling fear to one group while selling to someone else the reason they're afraid. "Oh, you're scared someone's going to kill you with a gun we sold them? Then here, let me sell you a gun."

Is Danielle's name starting to sound familiar? I know these things blur together. Who died when and where. Was it at a church? At a nightclub? At a school? Did they die with friends? Were they young? Old? Have families? How many were there at this one? Five? Ten? Twenty?

You can't learn all the names, not for every time it happens. They become numbers. So many at one place, so many at another. This one happened last week. Another one'll happen tomorrow.

Danielle taught at the school where a man broke through a side door and came in with three semi-automatic weapons sold by a company that donates part of its profits to your organization every year. They sponsor a big fundraiser for you even. I remember because when that actor was the president of your organization, he gave a big speech about the importance of owning guns. Found out later he had Alzheimer's. Probably had it most of the time he was the talkin' head for your group, and you knew it, and you did not care because he looked so good up talking. He'd been in those movies about the Bible, and he seemed so biblical, and people wanted to believe him so damn much.

Anyway, a man with guns he'd bought legally a week earlier walked through that school where Danielle worked and started shooting through closed doors. Through windows. The news showed the videos afterward. Him dressed in camo like he was headed to war.

You say "what stops a bad man with a gun is a good man with a gun." The school security guard, when he heard the shooting, he came running, and this man shot him in the face before he'd come all the way around the corner. And then he kept on firing.

You remember about the police, right? They arrived but they waited before going into the school. Ten minutes. Shots still going off. All those good men with guns, and none of them wanting to die that day.

Every kid now has a cell phone. Something like this happens, they call their parents, grandparents, whoever it is they love. They send text messages. They say they're scared. Terrified. Hearing guns. Hearing screaming. They're hearing people die. Not like in movies or video games. Real life is a different thing.

Danielle called me. I was at the hospital, visiting someone from the congregation. I let the call go to my voice mail.
Here. I'm going to play it. I want you to hear it. No, I want you to really and truly listen to it.

Stop crying. Just stop. Stop, and listen.

Do you hear that? Do you hear the screaming in the background? Do you hear that fear? You hear Danielle telling those children they're going to be okay? She's lying to them. She's lying because she knows it won't be okay.

Shut up. Just shut up. And. Listen.

This here's when she's praying. Praying to God to save these children. She never once says anything about herself. She prays for them.

And God doesn't save them. And neither does the good man with a gun.

Because you hear that? Gunfire, and more screaming, and then nothing.

The bullet ripped through her classroom door. Through Danielle. Shattered the phone.

Twenty-one dead that day.

I need to play it again. You can't know how many times I've listened to it. You can stand to listen to it twice. The screaming and crying and begging to God, then nothing.

You know, I don't think God was listening that day.

No, you shut up and listen. Because for me, I never stop hearing this. It is the only thing I've heard in my head since the day I played it back the first time. You will sit here and listen to everything that happened to my daughter and those children.

I wasn't right for a long time after. There was a funeral for Danielle, and she's buried back home. The whole thing killed my Carrie Ann. Doctors said it was cancer, but I know it was because she had no fight in her no more. She was gone in a year. I buried her next to Danielle.

I gave up preaching. It didn't seem right to go in front of people, tell 'em things about God I wasn't sure I believed no more.

Everyone made a big fuss of it for a bit, said we needed to change things, but in the end, we know no one's changing shit. There's too much money, and you've twined it up with people thinking the guns are what keep 'em free. What they don't see is how tethered they are to 'em. They're slaves to the companies you promote, to the politicians you pay for, to the products they buy.

Now you're wondering where this goes. I've done broken into your home, got a gun against your head, and you think, what now?

I'll tell you I only got one bullet in this gun. A gun that gives your organization money every year as a charitable donation. Ain't that almost funny? It is a little, you gotta admit.

Question is, do I use the bullet on you, act like getting rid of you'll change anything, or do I use it on me, so you can see what it is you're really selling. Somehow, I think it might be different, me standing three feet from your face. You understand what a bullet really does to a person. What it did to Danielle and those children.

Because you say you're about freedom and liberty and personal responsibility no matter what, but I'll tell you the cost of what it is you're selling is children and wives and husbands and loved ones. No one asked to die so you could tell people they need a gun in Target, but they're paying the cost for it anyway.

This here's when you try to convince me you value human life, and you ask me what kind of person do I take you for.

And I'll tell you we've already established that. Now we're just haggling over price.

Inspired by Eric Conrad's column "We're Just Haggling Over Price," published August 3, 2015, on the Huffington Post.

Art Young, "Eleven Hours a Day," ~1912

"She asks me if I know how to make it look like an accident."

Pretty Like
Money Can't Buy

AD Schweiss

The Dallas Ritz-Carlton might be the nicest place I ever seen. So nice it make me wish I live someplace like this. Once I kill this lady's brother, I'll at least stay here for a night sometime soon.

Walking into the lobby here, air feel like I left Dallas for some other planet. The air like somebody running winter fingertips on the small of your back. My skin go all tight and some lady standing beside a couple overstuffed chairs offer me a towel and when it touches my face it smell like vegetables and everybody walking around with jackets on like James Bond. It's even nicer than a La Quinta.

I'm in a pair of heels click like river rocks on the marble floor, like every person in here is on display for each other in one of those art museums. I wonder whether my brunette roots showing too bad or not because I pulled my hair back into a pony.

Walking through the lobby, nobody say, "Can I help you?" when what they really mean is "leave." This the kind of place where if you make it inside here, people know you didn't get in on accident.

When I get to the elevators there's carpet softer than some mattresses I slept on, and that must be why the hallway so quiet. I don't even have to put in a card for what floor I want. That's another thing: if you go to a rich person hotel like this, nobody worried you're going to go to the wrong floor. The elevator move so fast it's like I's being picked up by a giant in a fairytale who want to look at me close.

Sometimes I get a call about now, right before I's supposed to meet the client. Sometimes when the call comes, it's tears and the words come out faster than the client's lungs can work. Sometimes the client, she's too scared to hire me—to go through with killing somebody—and she cancel last second. Scared, I get.

But sometimes the client's got a voice that's cold and beat down and when she says, "I made a mistake," the voice remind me of spending nights with my daddy jacklighting deer from our truck when I was small, watching him shoot a buck from the open cab. Covering my ears and squeezing my eyes shut; praying he'd miss and praying we'd have food at the same time and praying it was over and praying Daddy wouldn't make me take the shot.

The women who cancel last minute are always the ones who want me to kill their husbands. And the clients who blame themselves—'*I made a mistake*'—they're the ones with husbands who deserve to get it the worst. Those women are like the deer in my daddy's spotlight, because I always prayed for those deer to run, even when I was the one taking my shot.

No call comes today, though. There a stillness in the hallways, a space that feel cleaner than bleach and smell like soap at one of them stores in the mall. I pass a table of ice-water with cucumber slices and real glass tumblers. Mostly the rich feeling come from the quiet. Cheap hotels, middle of the day, maids vacuuming one room or another with Mexican radio stations and them talking without lowering their voices to one another, or there's somebody holed up in their room with a TV they leave on all afternoon or a door open a crack, like they don't give a fuck if somebody look in on what they doing.

Most hotels they treat you like if you at a hotel in the middle of the day you not worth being polite to.

I knock on Room 601 and I pray I don't start the sweats. This lady ain't the police but that's exactly what I'd think if the police about to arrest me.

The lady who answer the door in Room 601 got lips shimmer like a lake with no boats on it, the color of her lip stain sharp as the slice in a wedding cake. Can't guess her age. She not young, but she got a dress that wrap her body close and make you guess at the shape underneath like the shadow of a mountain cat and she look like she could take off at a dead run right there in her heels or jump across a puddle.

She got fear in the corners of her mouth and the fear go all the way up to her eyes. I put on my voice like I's working a regular work job where you got to talk that fake-ass way: "Annette?"

I think she still worried I'm a cop when she let me in her room. This hotel room so big it got a separate part with a TV the size of a whiteboard like in school, and then there's a kitchen table set for four people.

Tug my blouse out. "Not wearing a wire. No gun." I reach into my pocket and pull out a folder knife I took off a nightstand once. "All I got's this, but that's mostly for my own protection." I smile when I say it, a *just between us girls* kind of smile.

That put her at ease only some, like a shelter dog on the first night in a house.

Twist up my eyebrows so I look kind of worried. "Can we sit? Sorry, but is that all right if we sit?" I point at my heels. With people this fancy you gotta ask for permission before you breathe practically, and apologize for things you're not sorry for.

She start in quick and gets talking easy like she got a lot to say.

"I'll never forget the look on his face," is what she say first.

She shows me a picture of her brother without me asking. That's how I know she want him dead bad. The picture still in the frame, and the brother and some older man, I'm guessing her daddy, they standing beside one of those airplanes that float on the water and smiling through sunburns like they just took over the world.

"We had all the paperwork out, about Daddy and the Trust. I asked my brother, 'Well, if you and Paula died, who would take Hazel?' and he *named some idiot he worked with*. I said, 'Brian, we're family. Family is *supposed to mean something.*' And then, I'll never forget the look on his face."

Annette's voice sour like flat Coke. She talk with her hands a bunch, palms out across the table toward me. Fingers dancing to get at the words. She got gel nails, not painted, sandy tan and natural-looking, buffed up slick and shiny catching the light. Make the air around her fingers look electric, like she holding a bolt of lightning. She got a ring with a diamond the size of a jolly rancher but it's the nails make her look rich.

If I ever had money? *Kill your brother* money? I'd get gel nails like Annette got.

Annette stare at the picture of her brother, run her thumb down the side of the picture frame. When she speak again, her voice get husky and mean like a football coach and I know she's talking how her brother sound in her head.

"'*I don't want you raising Hazel because you're bad with money, Annette.*' He said I'm going broke—which isn't true. He actually said that. I'm named as successor trustee if Brian dies and he's wanted me off the trust for years."

Thing about this client, Annette: she repeat herself. She told me this exact story on the phone when she hired me even though I interrupted her like, lady, you don't gotta tell me all this and don't say this stuff on the phone. Repeating herself even now, telling me how much private school cost for her own kids.

I don't tell Annette she repeating herself. I'm not stupid and she's paying me a whole bunch of money. But I make a note to check the bathroom before I go. I'm guessing she got pills.

Annette holding anger that crumble around the eyes and it's sad because she made those eyes up so pretty and it's only when she cry I see how much work goes into being that beautiful, with mascara run like gasoline into a gutter.

"It's so complicated sometimes, our family." This hotel got tissue boxes in silver holders, and there's a box on the coffee table so I offer one. When I hold out the tissue box to her she look at it for a second, a flash of that nasty *can I help you* look and she don't want to touch something that's in my hand. She take the tissue box but only barely.

Annette ask me if I know how to make it look like an accident. Edge in her voice hard as one of those metal credit cards—question and statement—the way she probably tell her dry cleaner how much starch her husband like in his shirts.

I nod like I used to when I's waiting tables. "Women always want it to look like an accident," I tell her, like I'm sharing some fact about Texas history or which direction geese fly. "And I only work for women."

I pull out a UPS envelope I picked up this morning from general delivery with a fake ID. We use a couple cheap Samsung phones to get her banking info through a VPN. Annette's phone—her regular phone, not the burners I bought—it chirp when she logs into her bank account from the burner, and she have to verify her ID by holding up her face to her phone.

As I get up to leave Annette tell me I cost less than her kindergartner's Montessori tuition. *What she want me to say to something like that?*

I say, "'Money well spent," but my smile so fake that my voice ring with hollow iron but that's okay because maybe she want to know she hired me for a bit of that fire. A little ding hit on my phone tell me I got paid the first half what she owe me. The little kitchen area of her hotel room got the microwave hidden behind a recessed wood panel. I cook the phones for ten seconds and take them both with me.

"Once it's done, I'll be in touch for the second half."

Annette say "thank you" because rich people always thanking you when they pay you.

I ask if I can use the bathroom before I go.

Annette leave her Xanax out where anybody can get at it and even if I had a billion dollars I would never be that dumb.

The hotel room door click shut when I walk out, just me and thick carpet, a quiet hallway, and a picture of the man I'm hired to kill in my mind. Annette's voice between my ears, thanking me and paying me and telling me about how difficult her life turned out to be.

◆

Annette's brother, Brian, he live in Denton. He wear denim workshirts and kiss his wife goodbye every morning. He drive a Toyota Tundra without a speck of dust on it, and Brian lives close enough to where he work that he don't have to drive on a freeway and when he drive his truck he let the windows down and keep his hair long like the guy in the Mission Impossible movies.

Never stops at bars on the way home.

But some mornings there's a high school track nearby where he lives. He go there and run the steps of a stadium before work like he trying out for a team or something, or like he trying to impress somebody. My mother would say he trim as a maiden and the sweat cling to him. He and Annette got the same lean frames, the way rich people got better things to do than eat.

I wait at the stadium where he do his running, get there early morning before the sun come up and keep my seatback laid down low so my Corolla look empty. That Toyota Tundra of his come roaring through the parking lot and when he walking toward the stadium he wearing a hoodie and some of those wireless headphones that go all the way in your ear.

He don't notice me until I'm behind him and I practically have to shout. I never been this close to him before, only followed him and seen him in pictures and he going gray at the temples, slush-in-a-parking-lot color in that maple hair. In some stray corner of my mind, I run fingers through that hair but in the parking lot I already got the gun trained on him and when he turn to face me there's enough light to see I's serious.

He take the headphones out and put his hands in front of his body. Fear sets his eyes to boil and I see how he and Annette are blood: a stillness in both their eyes, like they're both running scared—deer in a spotlight—and the same cracked-china frown from forehead all the way to the shoulders.

Brian smart. He lower one hand, gentle as a doe, and take a wallet from a little zip pocket on his shorts. He throw it my way without saying nothing and put the hand back up.

I keep the gun dead on his sternum. With my other hand I hold up my phone. I got a picture of his sister I took off Instagram and my phone light up the space between us because the sun still low on the horizon.

He look at the picture and it don't take too long to explain myself.

Brian don't even look surprised his sister trying to kill him and he don't take convincing to know this idn't some kind of joke. He just ask if we can sit down in the stadium a minute. I lower my gun but I stay outside arms reach and keep the gun away from him. If he try for my gun, I'll have time to get a shot off.

We walk over to where he does his running and sit in the bleachers beside the concrete steps. I sit on a spot of the bench marked "CC" and he sit by the steps, on "AA," and the spot between us far enough he can't get a hand on me.

I slide him my phone along the bench between us.

"Annette is always doing things like this." Brian look through the email between his sister and me. "She gets in over her head. Easily. Her plans are always, 'If I just spend a ton of money on *this* fund, or *that* business, then it'll fix all my problems,'" Brian got a tone in his voice like he told this story before and I figure he could probably go on like this a while if I let him. His eyes, same cold blue-gray eyes Annette got: all irritated at the edges from sweat and exercise and being pissed and having nowhere to put it.

Brian lets that hard stare look on past me toward the football field below us, first light on emerald plastic grass that won't ever die. I set my eye on the steps I watched Brian run this last week while I's tailing him. Brian and Annette both got that rich person kind of skinny where they don't even have any paunch to them and they look too old and too young all at once. I imagine if I ever get money like they got—do whatever I want money—I imagine myself running these steps and how I wouldn't even feel tired because I'd feel lighter than air.

Brian fans out his hands like he giving up, like he responsible for his sister and she having a wild season—not like she just tried to have him killed. "She bought farmland in Tennessee; *she didn't know how to manage it*. She bought an apartment complex—couldn't figure out why she'd gotten *such* a good deal on it. Never made a dime. She doesn't work and she doesn't really know how the world works, I guess."

I pull out two new Samsung burners, same kind I always use once before I crunch them up and fry them and put the pieces in four different counties. I got the screen pulled up so Brian realize it's time to put out. I put one of the phones on the bench where he can reach it.

"I was hired to kill you, Mr. McMurtrey," I say, using my fake on-the-phone voice like I'm trying to act all superior and shit. "But I am a *businesswoman*. Killing people is *expensive* and *messy*." I'm talking that way rich people talk where they say real basic shit but they pause like you're supposed to think about it.

Brian nod, like he understand the shake already. I keep on. This a speech I given before. "Double what she paid me, Mr. McMurtrey. And then I'll shoot your passenger windshield. You get in your car," and here I let a little bit of the hills in my voice, and I give my eyes just a little bit of gas so he knows what I am, "and drive like hell. You make the 9-1-1 call while you driving and say some *man* tried to shoot at you. You didn't get a good look. If you say it was a woman, I'll find out and then I *will* kill you, Mr. McMurtrey."

Brian's eyes going real sad over to where he got that nice Toyota parked, like I said I was going to shoot his dog.

"Then you're going to hire a private security guard for six months, Mr. McMurtrey, and you will tell your sister you've got a private investigator looking into who tried to kill you. That'll scare her, probably bad enough."

"And I don't go to the cops about you."

I take all the blood out of my face when I look back at him. Hold his gaze like an egg I'm fixing to smash on a windshield. 'If you go to the police, I'll kill you,' is one of those things where the more you say it out loud, the less people take you serious but when you think it without saying it, people know how much you mean it.

Instead, I say his daughter's name. And then I point at the phone and say a number.

"I don't have that kind of money on hand."

I point with the gun. "Prove it."

He pull up a Blackrock account and log in. "See? I'm limited to moving ten thousand a day."

I tell him set the phone down where I can see it, and I almost feel bad when he does what I say because it means end of the road for Brian McMurtrey.

I really ham it up, reading the screen like a lousy report card. I thumb the screen a little and point. "Says here, 'No daily transaction limit.'" I just made that up, but it sound like something a bank would say.

Brian look down at the phone and his brows knit together in a way that make me think—probably for the last time—how much he and Annette look like kin. While he distracted I bring the syringe down on his shoulder. I know there a spot in there where the muscles have thick layers and the injection hard to see on an autopsy.

Stuff in the syringe don't last long before it break down and it'll look like a heart attack when the coroner run a whole-blood assay. Brian's eyes meet mine and he react a second too slow. Makes a grab for me but his face go purple in the space of a heartbeat, color of a car-accident bruise, and he fold over at the gut like he straining on the toilet. Hands groping dumb on the bench in front of him, remind me of catfish flapping with too much fight on the deck of a boat and trying for a breath that ain't there.

I give him a push, just my hands on his chest but I drive the push with my hips. If I kick at Brian I might get shoe tread on his clothes. Leaving shoe tread in a crime scene is like a scratcher ticket for an FBI agent. Brian go down easy enough when I push him: the bleachers ring like church bells so I know he hit his head just right. His legs give a few kicks, a dog running after bunnies in his sleep or somebody trying to kickstart a bike, and he bring his arms up to his mouth before he go still. The last sound he make a pushing sound, air in puckered lips like he working hard for that last breath and I watch him a few seconds.

Gone.

I step back a bit and size up the way Brian's body lying. It'll fool a patrol cop and once you fool them, they tell the detective it's nothing, and then the detective tell the coroner it's nothing, and nobody wants to look for trouble somebody else said wasn't there.

Over on the bleacher where Brian and I were talking, Brian's phone still unlocked. Everything happened that fast. I don't even have to get close to read the screen and see those numbers.

Big numbers. The world spin a little while I count commas to make sure I'm seeing it correct. For a second, I try to imagine if it were all in hundred-dollar bills, how big would the stack be? Or, hell, if the money were in nice houses or airplanes, how many could I buy?

Numbers so big my mind just say, "No, get out of here with that," like I'm too poor to believe this kind of money could be real.

I know I need to leave before somebody arrive and find Brian's body but blood rings in my ears and I wish seeing this money thrilled me, but it didn't.

This kind of money scare me.

If I stole from somebody who couldn't afford it, nobody would notice. Could steal a checkbook—somebody's whole life savings—and they'd be lucky if a cop car get sent out. But Brian's money—the money I know is now *Annette's* money once the ink on the death certificate dries—I know if a penny go out of place they'd tear the skies and the ground apart just to bury me deeper than anybody could find.

I's panicking real bad. Wipe away tears and take the phone with me. Walking up them bleachers is hard now because my breath won't stay inside my body but next thing I know I'm behind the wheel of my rented Corolla and on the freeway, reciting the numbers from Brian's bank account. Miles pass by and I miss my exit.

I see them numbers staring at me when I'm on the road. For the rest of the day, every bite of food I eat taste empty, like the salt on my french fries a hundred miles away. When I close my eyes that night I think about that money and I imagine how if I tried running up the steps of a stadium my legs would move so fast I'd keep on running and launch up to the sky.

My motel room that night got a mattress sag real bad in the middle from all the bodies there before me. I can feel a spring against my back and I found a hair and I sleep on top the sheets. Them sheets scratch in the Denton heat and even the air conditioner know I'm too cheap to be worth trying to cool off.

In the dark, in that room, in my mind, I imagine having a body like Annette with lungs and a heart like a speedboat engine. Skin and muscles and no fat on my arms, just a machine pumping clean. I'd buy one house that would be mine and a hundred others just to rent to stupid people like me. I'd get those gel nails and I'd tip real big so the gals at the nail place would be nice to me right when I walk in.

◈

I call Annette two weeks after the funeral service and the obituary; I use VPN so it like the call coming from Germany instead of twenty miles away, and I don't put polish on my voice. The voice she hear *me*. *Real me*. I don't peg Annette as especially savvy but even she know that talking to the hitter after the job is done risky as hell.

"Morning, Annette."

The only words she gets out: "Is everything . . ." and she don't talk more, which is smart of her.

"Everything fine. Here's where we gonna meet." I wonder whether she can hear the smile in my voice.

◈

Annette park at the Dairy Queen like I told her and I should have had her get me something because I been sitting here so long. When I'm rich I wonder whether dip cones still gonna taste good. Probably they won't.

Can see Annette real clear from the second floor of this motel, good LED floodlights in the parking lot. There's this way Annette walk, even when she don't know somebody watching: she *strut* like she meeting somebody important with iron in her calves to make the world rise up to meet her.

I think about all the things make Annette pretty like money can't buy:

Pretty like me watching her walking into a place like she own it, and never eating Jack in the Box or even wanting to. I watch her get close to the steps that lead her up to the walkway outside my room.

I think about the way a hoodie and jeans fit nicer when you're beautiful and your stomach real tight.

Annette knock real gentle like a momma with a baby sleeping inside and when I open the door she got a smile that don't hit her eyes and I figure a lot of people when they hire me, they find out I didn't fix all their problems. Annette's mouth don't crease in the corner from toothaches and boyfriends and you can't buy that kind of pretty but you don't get it without the kind of money Annette got.

I got the lights on, and the phones already set up on the bed. Annette got no makeup on but her skin smells better than perfume.

I got Annette's Xanax pills all splayed out on the bed like a good night gone too far and I chopped one of them up in a neat rail and Annette look at my hand and the smile wilt away and when you rich like Annette you get to trust people, I suppose, because you never have to meet people like me mostly.

She even scream like something out of a movie but she trust people too much so I guess I got a good lead on her. The wind go out quick when I hit her stomach and she in good shape but she can't fight even though she try.

Putting her down is hard because I have to avoid hitting the face. Need her face pretty to unlock her phone.

This motel real good because it got Wi-Fi, and I use that to connect to that same Blackrock account Brian showed me, except now it showing Annette's name at the top of the screen. I rented this room in Annette's name, too, and the motel got a pool that nobody uses but somebody gonna find her there. We're three counties over from where I killed Brian. That way she won't get the same coroner.

❖

That afternoon I switch cars and I'll switch cars twice before I get where I'm going. Mostly while I'm driving I try not to eat because I need to stop eating junk and start eating clean like rich people. I drive the speed limit with two hands on the wheel.

One of my knuckles raised just a little, on the same hand where I got a nail chipped from where Annette tried to hold on for just a minute before the lights went out. I look at that chip in my nail whole time I drive and it's driving me crazy, glinting in the sun.

I'll stop at a nail shop, once I get where I's going. My nails gonna look pretty when they done.

“It's a classic Horatio Alger story backdropped
by state-sanctioned violence in humid locales—as
profoundly American as Cheez-Whiz and gun crime.”

God's Way of Hiding in the Shadows

Thomas Trang

Bannerman spent that morning in the suburbs of Dallas picking through the garbage of a retired US Marine named Stanley Northrop—the fourth name on a list of seven. By late afternoon, he was in a lab downtown off the 75 confirming a positive DNA match. Bannerman called the client soon after, then made his way to Fort Worth Airport. The client's security team met him on the tarmac. A pair of Rapa Nui-jawed lunkheads straight out of central casting—all tight buzzcuts and dark Boss suits—they hustled him onto a converted Boeing 737 with the square footage of a two-bed apartment in Manhattan and the interior design aesthetic of a Saudi prince. It was wheels up at sundown, a fading burnt peach glow on the edge of the horizon.

Fifteen minutes after take-off, the security guards tried to kill him with a wire garrote.

There was a brief but tense scuffle, with Bannerman grabbing a holstered weapon from one of the guards and shooting him in the arm, then the other one through the knee, and finishing off with a third bullet that cracked a window. This led to a slow but irreparable loss of cabin pressure as the private jet began its swan dive through the Texas night toward a cotton field somewhere north of Lubbock.

Things had gotten out of control.

❖

It was all good just a week ago.

The client came through one of his usual handlers. The job was lucrative, freighted with moral turpitude and the prospect of illegal behavior. Nothing he couldn't manage. Nothing he hadn't done before, often in service to the federal government for higher geopolitical stakes, but much less money.

Bannerman met with the client at Big Pix HQ in Culver City, waiting in the lobby underneath the company's green and yellow logo and a ninety-foot screen broadcasting a loop of promo stills from next summer's programming schedule. A young Black kid dressed in steampunk cosplay chic took him upstairs to Luisa Rovayo's office. She motioned for Bannerman to sit down in a vintage Eames chair the color of sun-faded cocoa while she wrapped up a call. Her smile was dazzling and suggestive of orthodontic rigor.

She apologized for insisting on the meeting. "I know you prefer to work anonymously, but the truth is I wanted to meet with you in person. Get a feel for you. Call it a gut check. That's how I like to do things. There are risks involved, but it's an approach which has served me well so far. You come highly recommended, Mr. Bannerman."

Luisa Rovayo—fiftysomething with a beauty pageant attractiveness that retained its luster through clean living and exotic skincare. Bannerman isn't an industry guy. He doesn't follow the trades. He barely watches TV anymore beyond channel surfing in hotel rooms between gigs, but she has enough of a public profile for him to already know who she is.

Her official title is Head of Content Acquisition & Strategy at Big Pix, but the worst kept secret in Hollywood? Rovayo is the real shot-caller inside the media giant these days.

A war orphan adopted by two aid workers in Chile in the aftermath of the 1973 coup and brought back to San Diego, Rovayo initially struggled at school. She wrestled with English up until her teenage years, but taught herself the language through reruns of *The Love Boat* and *Remington Steele*. She graduated from Cal State with a communications degree and started in the business as an assistant at CBS reading through the slush pile.

For the next seven years she worked her way up the ladder, first as a script doctor with a keen eye for story dynamics and nascent cultural trends before moving over to Universal in a management role. Rovayo surprised everyone when she joined Big Pix in 2010 as an executive VP with generous stock options. Once streaming took off, she was put in charge of building out the company's original content. Her rise was meteoric. She drew showrunners away from the traditional networks with exclusive development deals worth millions on the strength of nothing more than a two-page treatment in some cases—unheard of at the time.

It was an expensive gamble that paid off. Big Pix reconfigured the landscape of television within a decade in the same way a drug dealer would flood the market. Romantic comedies about salmon farms in Alaska, hawkish military dramas based in Yemen, stand-up comedy specials that feted third-rate hacks as *artistes*, and lurid reality shows set on faraway tropical islands.

Something for everyone, and Rovayo had a hand in all of it. She lived by algorithm numbers and the wisdom of crowds. It was impossible to pin down her aesthetic beyond the desire to reach as many eyeballs as possible.

But if her tastes were wide, her vision was curiously specific. The rumor is she remains very hands on to this day—from scripts and dialogue through to story development and right down into casting choices and costume design. Whether she sleeps is open to fierce debate.

To be anointed by Luisa Rovayo would put you on the road to success, but she would always be there as a backseat driver. It's a compromise many aspiring creatives are willing to make.

Sell me your dream. That was the line she always used in development meetings.

It became the title of an infamous profile in the *New Yorker* three years ago. The piece also detailed rumors of hardball negotiating tactics and cut-throat business acumen. There was talk of IP infringement and hushed-up out-of-court settlements. Some former employees hinted at a ferocious temper and borderline sociopathic tendencies. Most of them refused to comment.

Go down the Reddit-hole, you'll find dozens of conspiracy threads on how her shows are designed to indoctrinate the viewer into a cynical and power-driven strain of social conservatism. Her corseted historical dramas and gritty neo-noir procedurals are sprinkled with coded allusions to reactionary thinkers like Emil Cioran and Murray Rothbard. Dig even deeper online and there are Illuminati-tinged theories claiming she is a planted agent of chaos by the Rothschilds, the House of Windsor, or an alien race of lizards. Maybe all three.

But here are the facts.

Rovayo now controls an annual budget that's equivalent to the GDP of Zimbabwe.

Last year she was ranked 12th on *Fortune*'s Most Powerful Women list.

Those stock options with Big Pix have quintupled her net worth.

She's come a long way from that orphanage on the outskirts of Santiago.

It's a classic Horatio Alger story backdropped by state-sanctioned violence in humid locales—as profoundly American as Cheez-Whiz and gun crime. In a world of artfully curated public image and pampered Hollywood nepo-babies fast-tracked into success on either side of the camera, the unlikely fairy tale of Luisa Rovayo comes with an air of dark mystery. Perhaps even some danger.

It's the main reason Bannerman agreed to the job.

◈

Now he's walking into a motel reception office on the outskirts of Lubbock. It's the other side of midnight and Bannerman looks like refried dogshit. Falling out of the sky will do that to you.

He glances around the room while he waits. There are faded brochures for the Buddy Holly Center and the Science Museum on the counter. Crinkled PVC blinds cover the window. The faint sizzling sound from a neon sign outside throws a small pool of electric blue light on the car park, which is empty except for a dirty Subaru hatchback. The whole vibe of the place is like an Edward Hopper painting, with all of the surreal and poetic loneliness dropkicked into the 21st century.

The vibe *he's* going for with the woman on the front desk—someone at the tail end of a long night just looking for a place to sleep it off. Someone who might smoke in bed and abuse the ice machine privileges. Not exactly trustworthy but far from trouble.

Definitely not someone who just crash-landed a Boeing 737 twenty miles north of here, stole a Chevy pick-up from a farmhouse nearby, then hotfooted it back to civilization.

No siree Bob.

He pays in cash.

◈

Bannerman's room is on the first floor. He keeps the lights off and lays out on the bed, the adrenaline finally powering down. Every impulse tells him he should be moving, getting as far away from Lubbock as possible. The cops could already be onto the Chevy. Still . . . he needs to work out what he's up against. Rovayo's people will be all over Texas like chicken-fried steak once they realize he's not part of the plane wreckage.

So he sets himself up as bait. If they're good, they'll be cautious. Wait for him to drop his guard and move. It won't change anything. Bannerman still has the drop on *them*. But the next twenty-four hours will be tough, however it shakes out.

He checks his pulse and closes his eyes. Sleep washes over him like a rainstorm.

Muscle memory and training keeps it light.

Gentle footsteps on the landing wake him with a jolt.

The digital bedside clock reads a few minutes after five. It's still dark out. Nobody comes back to a Super 8 at this hour of the morning and moves with ninja-like stealth.

They're standing in front of his room now. The faded chrome handle turns and then slips back into place. Always worth a try. There's a moment of pregnant silence before a heavy foot kicks through the lock. A bear-framed silhouette fills the doorway, arms extended in a shooter's pose. Two shots from a handgun with a silencer attached, the sound like a robot cracking its knuckles. Geysers of cheap polyfoam spit upward from the mattress.

Bannerman rolls out from under the bed and charges at them in a single graceful movement, optimizing the element of surprise. Their bodies clash and bounce around the enclosed space as if locked in a demented tango. The shooter tries to swing his arm around and get another shot off. It's all the opening Bannerman needs. An elbow to the face, then his hands are on his neck squeezing the carotid arteries.

The man thrashes wildly like a fish out of water for a brief moment and then his body goes limp. Bannerman eases him onto the carpet with something approaching tenderness then searches through his pockets.

Six hundred dollars in crisp notes. A burner phone.

Bannerman moves toward the door. He waits, listens. Nothing. Then he makes his way along the first floor landing crouched low. Hunters nearly always move in pairs.

He finds the second one around the side of the Super 8 behind the wheel of an idled Lincoln Town Car. A few minutes pass before the driver gets out to check on his partner. He steps out of the Lincoln and starts to reach for his weapon, but Bannerman leaps forward from behind him and gets the guy in a tight chokehold. It puts him down.

Now he's behind the wheel himself, fishtailing it out of the car park heading south toward Lubbock. Bannerman looks inside the glove box. There's a pack of Marlboros and a chrome Zippo. He lights one and exhales, passing Shallowater on his left as sunrise tints the edge of a murky grey sky.

The burner phone rings. An unlisted number.

"Is it done?"

A familiar voice. Female.

Bannerman waits. Then he says, "Sure. In a manner of speaking."

Rovayo hangs up.

❖

He dumps the Lincoln on Broadway two blocks west of the Greyhound depot, and leaves the phone behind too. From there, Bannerman walks down Avenue K and kills an hour drinking black coffee in a diner before everything else opens up for the day. He keeps moving south and finds a cell phone shop, then buys himself a prepaid with one of the Benjamins from the hitter's pocket.

Bannerman makes the call to Kessler. "Everything okay there?"

"You tell me. I'm watching the news about how the company's private jet had to make an emergency landing in Texas last night, and now you're calling me first thing in the morning from an unknown number. Correlation doesn't always imply causation, but I have to assume the two are related."

"Things went sideways."

"Anything you need, brother."

Bannerman gives him a list.

Kessler reels off an address on the other side of Lubbock.

"He'll have a set of wheels for you. Totally clean." There's a pause then Kessler says, "The other stuff . . . how soon can you get to Albuquerque?"

"Tonight."

Kessler gives him the name of a hotel. "It'll be ready in six hours."

Kessler's word is bond. There's a room key for a suite waiting for Bannerman at Parq Central reception when he gets there a little after seven that evening. The woman behind the desk smiles as she hands it to him, saying, "Mr. Kessler is waiting on the roof deck."

Bannerman's worked with Roland Kessler almost fifteen years. Panhandle-raised peckerwood who made his bones as a broker for the mob in New Orleans. These days the dude is transnational; still . . . you can take the man out of the gator swamp, but you can't remove the monster from the man. He's pure southern hospitality on the outside, with all the warmth of a cobra beneath the surface.

"I told you this one was a pass. The vibe was off from the beginning."

"Who is Northrop? Has to be her father, right?"

"Northrop wasn't even his real name."

Bannerman clocks the past tense.

Kessler nods. "An electrical fire. Cops found him early this morning. Faulty wiring. That's what Dallas PD are saying for now. Hell of a tragedy."

"Hell of a coincidence."

"You know what Einstein called coincidence? *God's way of hiding in the shadows.*"

"God ain't got nothing to do with this."

"You should've passed on the job. You know what your problem is? Too blinded by the lights of Hollywood. All the bullshit glamor and celebrity. This stuff excites you."

"You think the story about the fire will hold?"

Kessler shrugs. "Who knows. Doesn't matter to us anyway. DPD won't release the body without a good reason, and Rovayo won't be submitting to a DNA test. The more I look at this, it ain't about wanting him dead. Not really. The shit she's into right now, she'd need some pretty good reasons just to keep him alive. The guy's name was Robert Joyce. Turns out he *was* ex-military, only not some regular jarhead. We're talking serious black ops."

"How do you know all this?"

"You think Stevie Ray was the only motherfucker pulling strings in Texas? I got people in San Antonio with access to all kinds of top-secret military shit. You shoulda ran the details by me first, instead of running off to L.A. like some fuckin' rube with a casting audition."

Kessler slides a manila folder across the table like he's dealing a blackjack hand.

"Take a look for yourself, you want to know what this is about."

Bannerman starts reading. The file goes back more than fifty years. Northrop was part of a covert team operating in Chile in tandem with the CIA. At some point, he went off the reservation and was discharged under a cloud of suspicion. There were rumors he was selling weapons to various paramilitary groups with Marxist tendencies across Latin America. After that, Northrop went AWOL and was out in the wilderness for years until he was picked up trying to cross the border at Nogales in 1998. Langley intel had him working security for Columbian drug barons by then.

"No wonder she doesn't want him in her life," he says.

Kessler laughs. "It's much bigger than whatever daddy issues she might have. The word in Tinseltown right now is that your friend Luisa Rovayo is spearheading a group of investors making a play to buy NBC."

"The network?"

"No, the cucumber farm. The fuck you think? Remember all that talk from Big Pix about disrupting legacy media? Turns out Rovayo's goal is a little more traditional. All she really wants is *more*. They fold the streaming into broadcast TV, and it's a game changer. She's already got Goldman on board, plus Chinese and *A-rab* funding, but the old man is a potential liability if it's her name on the masthead. This kind of deal, you're talking a high-altitude tightrope walk juggling balls of fire. The smallest thing knocks you off balance and it's over. This deal would put her on another level. We're talking *rich* rich. Shooting rockets into space and buying up chunks of New Zealand for the apocalypse type shit. How many bodies do you think that's worth to her? Plus these new media types, they're another species. They spend their whole lives in a world of make-believe. We're not talking about steel tycoons or even JP fuckin' Morgan here. Those guys still had a foot in the real world at least. Don't even get me started on these crypto assholes. But some shit never changes. That kind of money and power, people don't look much like people anymore. Only pieces on a board. Sacrifice a few pawns to capture the king? I doubt she'd even blink at the idea. That's the game being played. What I want to know is how you're gonna handle it."

Bannerman pushes the manila folder back across the table. "I'm playing a different game."

◈

Rovayo has been holed up in the foothills of Camelback Mountain on the outskirts of Phoenix about a week now. The house is set into the ochre sandstone as if it had been there since the dawn of time. He's watching from the peak, tucked between two boulders and camouflaged by scrub. Walls of floor-to-ceiling glass look out over an infinity pool. Three security guards are doing circuits around the perimeter at staggered intervals. Dusk hits, and the setting sun paints an apron of fire and shadow across the landscape. He'll make his move after dark.

Rovayo comes upstairs and finds him waiting in the master bedroom.

There's a moment of sudden blood-freezing terror before instinct takes over and she screams for the guards. She turns and runs down the hallway, kicking off designer slippers, taking the stairs two or three at a time before losing her balance. She trips and crumples up into a tangle of limbs and her overpriced Gucci kaftan.

Bannerman racks the slide of the Glock 17. That sound always makes the world drop an octave. He takes his time. He sits down on the steps beside her, slumped like Rodin's *Thinker*. The gun is in his left hand. "Your security is lax."

"You killed them?"

He shakes his head. "They're only doing their job. Soldiers. I can respect that."

"You served?" Rovayo straightens herself up and leans back against the wall.

"A long time ago. There's a lot more money in private contracting. I leveled up is all."

She lets out a deep groan. "I think I've twisted my ankle."

"You want to know the crazy thing? I would have clipped this guy myself if that was the job. And it wouldn't have been a house fire either. Too many variables on a stunt like that, plus you got these arson investigators out here like fuckin' Colombo. Someone that age, make it look like a heart attack. Pick your poison. Nobody'll think twice about it. For someone so successful, you're not very smart."

Rovayo offers up a grim and jagged laugh.

"There's a lot of that going around," she says. "All these tech bros living off imaginary wealth and buying up things they don't understand. Then they start wondering why it falls apart. Twenty something years in this business, and I know it way better than any of these guys sitting at the top. I figured it was my time."

"You sound greedy."

"It's like you said. *Leveling up.* Nobody was gonna just hand it over. But I had to make sure it was done right. Cross the T's, dot the I's. Plan for all the different contingencies. I'm not just talking about the funding. No loose ends."

Bannerman reaches for his cigarettes.

Rovayo says, "You got one for me?"

He gives her the pack. She takes one and puts it in her mouth.

He lights it for her and says, "You know those things'll kill you."

She smiles, despite herself. "So this is what you do, huh?"

"I've done it all, lady. Wet work, corporate espionage. I've run logistics on extortion jobs that reshaped the leadership of aerospace companies in Europe and brought down governments in Africa. I've crashed global oil prices. *Twice.* All this Hollywood black bag stuff, running stalkers out of town and smoothing over drug busts for Nickelodeon stars once they've gone off the rails? We're talking easy money for a couple of days' work. But with my skill set? It's a little like Orson Welles directing Geico commercials."

Rovayo exhales a thin plume of smoke then closes her eyes.

"Sounds like one hell of a TV show."

"I've often thought the same thing."

"It's still not too late."

"I don't know the first thing about television."

"What's to know?" Rovayo says. "You've already got all the stories, right? All you need to do is put it down on paper. We could even sit in a room, just the two of us, sketch out a few ideas to get started. Figure out the plot points. Identify the hook."

"You're crazy."

"No, I'm serious." She gets more animated as the plan takes shape. "Listen to me. *Semper Fi* is in its last season, so a zeitgeisty action-thriller type of show would fit perfectly with the schedule next year. This is exactly the thing we're missing. Think *24* or *Burn Notice*, only bigger. Something with real international reach. It's all about breaking into the foreign markets now. Something that taps into the mood of the audience. All their cynicism and paranoia about the modern world wrapped up in a propulsive story. There are a lot of ways this could work. I'm thinking a *case of the week* structure, kicking ass and taking names in exotic locations, but there could still be an underlying narrative thread that runs through the season. A puppet master pulling the strings. Maybe the sempai who's gone rogue. Maybe we even add a love interest. An old flame working for the other side. Something to generate more conflict."

Rovayo is in a pitch meeting for her life.

"We could fast-track development and production," she says. "I call in some favors, get a cast and crew in place, and we'd be filming by the end of the year once we've got a script locked down. I'd pay for the rights, get you on as a technical advisor, even throw you an EP credit. That's only fair. Just think about it. Easy money."

Bannerman grins. He lowers the Glock. "Okay, I'm listening. Sell me your dream."

"'Viva la nut cheese. I want to bathe in it.'"

Sin Carne

Eddie McNamara & Meirav Devash

Two hours into their open-air dinner under twinkling string lights, Tyler leaned back in his chair and watched his date sip a glass of very expensive unfiltered natural red wine. Sin Carne, the "it" restaurant of the moment served heirloom-variety plant-based foods on a boat anchored off a pier in Brooklyn Bridge Park with a sensational view of Manhattan.

Noa, the curvaceous redhead seated across from him, said she hadn't eaten "anything with a face" since, at the age of three, she found out that a cute yellow chick and a chicken nugget were the same thing. It was a sweet story, and when she told it, she laughed in an unrestrained way that was contagious. They were well into their second bottle.

Behind Tyler's amused chuckle was a desperate desire to know what she thought. Noa had nibbled her way through seven courses of his tasting menu and had yet to comment on the food. Tyler wasn't used to this type of withholding. His restaurant had a six-month waitlist for a two-top and universal love from the food media. He was a made-for-television rock n' roll chef, complete with a tattooed neck and hands.

Their server placed a family-size order of raw lasagna on the table—a stack of uncooked, thinly-sliced zucchini ribbons layered with nut-based cream, dehydrated tomatoes, and fresh micro basil, accompanied by a long-winded explanation.

Noa cut a tiny end piece and chewed. Her face lit up. "That was the most delicious bite of food I've ever tasted," she said. And then she burst into peals of laughter. She pointed at words on the chalk menu board hanging above the bar.

"Nut cheese?! Can anyone say that without laughing like a 10-year-old?"

Tyler's smile vanished. He laid his large, graffitied hand on top of Noa's small, pristine one. Their first physical contact of the evening was electric and commanded her attention. She took another bite and stared into Tyler's eyes.

"I use macadamias and cashews for the base," he said. "For a cheese-like richness. Then, I add nutritional yeast, Himalayan salt, and a little yuzu for depth."

"You're a genius. I take back everything I said about nut cheese. Viva la nut cheese. I want to bathe in it."

"I know a guy who might be able to make that happen for you," Tyler said before snorting and covering his face with his hands. "Oh God, that's awful. I'm sorry. I don't even know what I'm saying anymore—that's how into you I am tonight, Noa. Where have you been all my life?"

"We're new to the city," she said.

"Moved for your job?"

"No. Nothing like that," said Noa. "More like a fresh start. My husband and I had to leave Providence in a bit of a hurry. There was this whole thing with a guy named Matteo." She rolled her eyes.

"Do I need to worry about this husband, or do you have some kind of arrangement?"

Noa exhaled. "Yes and yes, actually. Let's make sure we don't get caught."

"Is it an open relationship?" he asked.

"As far as I'm concerned it is."

"OK, but does your husband agree with your interpretation?"

"He's more of a 'don't ask, don't tell' kind of guy. Old school," she said.

"Oh," Tyler said. "I . . . well, Lizette and I have an ethically non-monogamous relationship. That's how we play."

"My guy doesn't go for that hippie shit. He thinks of himself as an alpha male."

"But you know better?" Tyler said.

"How much longer do you want to talk about my husband?" Noa asked. She let go of her fork, and it clattered on her plate. Pouting, she asked, "What's next?"

"China White has that dark '80s party tonight," he said. "It's great for dancing or people-watching."

They stumbled out of Sin Carne. Tyler spotted a limo driver idling in front of the restaurant while his riders dined inside. He was willing to take them to Chinatown for 50 bucks, but Tyler talked him down to 35 before they hopped in. Noa pulled an engraved silver flask out of her handbag and took a big, smooth swig before passing it to Tyler. He flinched from the throat-burning hooch a bum might drink out of a paper bag.

They arrived at China White; a kitschy chop suey tourist trap turned underground party space. The walls were covered with crimson Victorian opium-den wallpaper and intricate hand-painted gold filigree. Though the lighting was low, the open drug use would shock even a club kid from the actual '80s. The bartender ignored the three-deep line of customers and went straight to Tyler. He ordered a double Chivas and a vodka tonic.

"On the house," the bartender said, flicking his neon visor sunglasses. Noa swallowed the scotch in one shot, grabbed Tyler's face with both hands and kissed him on the forehead.

"Fuck, yes. Now do a bump with me," she said, holding the back of her hand—and the tiny pile of white powder—under his nose.

"What is it?" he asked.

"There's only one way to find out. Maybe it's coke. Maybe it's Molly. Let's have an adventure."

Tyler grinned and snorted the mystery powder. She replenished it and sniffed some herself. They shared a 10-minute ketamine coma. Joy Division's "She's Lost Control" came on and they felt a reckless urge to dance. So, they did, until she playfully bit his bottom lip and pulled him by his tie, like a dog on a leash, to a table where they sat.

Tyler's thoughts were hazy from the drugs. He couldn't watch her dangle that Louboutin high-heeled pump off the end of her foot for one more second. So, she liked alpha males. He grabbed her by the back of the neck and whispered in her ear.

"You're going to get up and walk straight into the men's room. You're going to wait for me in the back stall until I come in there and tear you apart."

She ran her hand along his arm and removed his hand from the back of her neck.

"What makes you think I'm the kind of girl who'd fuck you in a nightclub bathroom?" she asked.

Oh shit. Tyler had embarrassed himself. He didn't know how to answer without making this any worse.

"Don't you have to inform Lizette before you take me? Mr. Ethical Non-Monogamy?"

Tyler felt exposed. He looked away from Noa and felt his face burn.

Noa stood. She spun and walked away, her hips swaying dramatically, accentuating her curves. She looked back over her shoulder at him with a mischievous glint in her eye. Then she made her way in the direction of the men's room.

Relieved, Tyler got up and followed her trail into the restroom. He passed one guy washing his hands and two dudes at the urinals. He opened the door to the last stall and found Noa.

He hiked her dress up and lifted her off the ground. This was the reason he did so many squats at the gym. She wrapped her legs around him as he pressed her against the tiled back wall. They kissed with the passion of a couple hate-fucking. Noa grabbed his right hand and wrapped it around her throat. "You know what to do," she said. He squeezed the sides of her neck.

"Choke me like you fucking mean it," she whispered. She glared at him.

She wore a pained expression like she was struggling to breathe, but Tyler knew not to let up. She wanted to disappear into white noise, to test her boundaries. He watched her beautiful face with interest as he fucked her. She couldn't make a sound because she couldn't breathe. Her cheeks, once pink and flushed, began to turn a shade of purple. Tyler started to release his grip, but she took her hands and held his choke in place.

Tyler forgot where he was until he felt her squeezing and contracting around his cock. He came in waves. The euphoria seemed to last forever. She let go of his hands and he let go of her neck. She gasped for air.

Soon they were back at the bar, sharing a cigarette Noa had stashed in her purse. "I don't smoke," she started to explain. "It's a dirty habit."

"Dirty habit, dirty girl," Tyler said, looking her up and down.

"I'll be your dirty girl," she said, "while your cum's inside me."

Tyler's phone vibrated in his pocket. He pulled it out. Lizette. He showed Noa and shrugged in resignation, killing the moment that bloomed between them.

"I should take this," he said.

"You should," she said. "I should head home before it gets late and he gets suspicious."

❖

In the back of her Uber Black car, Noa texted her husband.

Crisis averted. Secured a venue for the charity gala. Impressive guest list. Be home in 20. Xoxo.

Next, she picked up her phone and looked for Matteo's name in her contacts. His number was saved under the name Susan Richards. If she cared about Matteo, she'd call and check on him. She was glad she didn't have to hear his annoying Italian accent anymore. She texted.

Are you ghosting me? It's not like I want to see you again, but please have the human decency to let me know you haven't fallen off the planet.

The car arrived home without a response to either text. She entered her brownstone as quietly as possible, but there was always a loud creak outside the bedroom door. Damon was supposed to get that fixed. She crept into the room.

He was sitting on the bed, fully awake and fully dressed.

"Sorry for not calling," she said. "I was in a flow state."

"Anything you want to tell me?"

"Yes," she said. "I nailed down Brooklyn Bridge Park for the gala. A rising star chef is doing the menu."

He exhaled. "Congrats, babe," he said. "Now, come over here and gimme a kiss goodnight."

Noa approached, intending to give him a smooch on the head, but he pulled her towards him and onto the bed. Damon kissed her full on the mouth and ran his hand between her thighs. She stiffened.

"What is that smell?" he asked.

"Oh, I had a celebratory scotch with the team. Just one."

Damon sat up. "Right. I can smell the booze on your breath, but that's not it."

"Oh Jesus," she said. "Not this jealous shit again."

"It's not your smell. It's a musky smell. A manly smell."

"What, are you a bloodhound now?" Noa asked. "You should hear how ridiculous you sound."

She stood and adjusted her dress. "I work at a dog rescue. I had my arms around quite a few dogs today. Is that what you're talking about?"

"No."

"Fuck you, Damon," she said. She started walking toward the bathroom.

"Dogs don't wear cologne," he shouted. He grabbed her by the hair and pulled her back down onto the bed. "Don't you fucking lie to me. I know what you were doing. You can't help yourself."

She tried to deny his accusations. He rag-dolled her onto her back and choked her, wrapping his right hand around her throat. Her windpipe was restricted and she couldn't speak. Damon tightened his grip. Noa dug her nails into his arm in an act of desperation. The room darkened around the edges until everything went black.

When she awoke seconds later, feeling a simultaneous sense of confusion and calm. She scanned the room and saw Damon walking towards the living room. She scurried to the bathroom and slammed the door shut.

Damon made his way over to Noa's laptop. He listened to make sure the shower was running. He examined her search history. She had looked up Sin Carne, which means "without meat" in Spanish. It was also the name of the restaurant off of Brooklyn Bridge Park. This checked out with her story. Everything else in her history was her usual Instagram dog bullshit. And endless browsing for lingerie that she puts in her cart but never pulls the trigger and buys. If he didn't hate her so much, he would have surprise-ordered her wish list. She looked fantastic in lingerie.

Damon texted his assistant, Sara.

I need a table at Sin Carne ASAP. Use my father's name if you must.

❖

Tyler waited in the front of his restaurant to greet the 9:30 chef's table reservation—a solo diner and last-minute addition: Mob boss Giacomo "Greaser Jack" Fortunato's son, Damon. He arrived wearing a navy-blue suit with a crisp white dress shirt and no tie. Tyler stood with his hand outstretched. Damon bypassed Tyler's handshake and went in for a bro hug.

"I can't thank you enough for accommodating me," Damon said. "You didn't have to. My wife can't stop talking about the meal she had here with the girls from her work. I had to pull a couple of strings and experience it for myself. I hope you don't mind."

Tyler grinned wide. "No way, man. I'm psyched to have you."

He escorted Damon through the packed dining room. The chef didn't stop to chat, but he waved to his diners and fans as he continued through the kitchen door. The elevated chef's table was an arm's length from the garde manger station.

The line at Sin Carne operated more like a graceful ballet in a pristine laboratory than the hectic, shouty mosh pit of line cooks Damon was expecting.

"This is a class operation," he said under his breath, loud enough in that silent kitchen for Tyler to hear.

"Thanks, man." The chef placed a glass of wine in front of Damon along with a plate of three cherry tomatoes he smoked for 24 hours.

Damon took a bite and slammed his palm on the tabletop so hard that a startled sous chef dropped the tweezers they were using to garnish the plates with microgreens.

"These little tomatoes taste like Chinatown pork buns. This is just tomatoes? Nothing else?" he asked.

"Just tomatoes and smoke, Mr. Fortunato," Tyler said. "The time under temperature brings out their sweetness. Many people think they taste pimentón or Spanish paprika, but I'll tell you the truth—it's only smoked tomatoes."

"Unbelievable," Damon said. "Get another bottle of this wine for the table. I'm gonna buy a case when I get home."

Tyler delivered course after course to Damon's table. On his second bottle of wine, Damon insisted Tyler sit with him. Tyler was surprised by how charming and intelligent Damon Fortunato was. They talked about travel and restaurants while polishing off two more bottles of wine.

"Tyler," Damon said, "I want to bankroll your expansion to Los Angeles, Seattle, Portland, Austin, Tokyo. If you can replicate this operation in those cities, you'll be the heaviest-hitting new chef in the industry. I tasted the future of food tonight and I want to buy into that future."

"Look, with all due respect, Mr. Fortunato—"

Damon cut him off. "What's this 'all due respect' bullshit? I know that you know my father, but I'm not in that line of work. I'm not some psychopath who needs an 'all due respect' stroke job. I'm in hospitality property development. I've got some locations that would be fantastic for Sin Carne. That's all."

"I'm not interested in being beholden to a hospitality group. I'm not a TV chef anymore. I did that to get this place going, but no more," said Damon. "I'm happy cooking here. My investors are paid off. I have no stress. I like it this way."

"Tyler. If my old man wasn't leaning on you for protection money every week, you wouldn't know who the fuck I was. That means there would be no way I'd get the chef's table on a few hours' notice. Let's stop bullshitting each other," Damon said.

"You've got me all wrong, Mr. F—"

"Call me Mr. Fortunato one more time," said Damon.

"What?"

"Tyler, I get it. You don't trust me. Allow me to prove that I'm a valuable friend to have. I know for a fact you've got some Staten Island goon representing my old man coming to you every week for an envelope with the pizzo in it. A chef with broken hands is useless, so you play the game and pay. I can make sure that guy never bothers you again. I'm asking for a meeting, not a yes."

"You serious?"

"Dead serious, Tyler," Damon said. "That's how much I believe in you."

◆

It was a beautiful night. Guests at the annual Animal Protection and Rescue gala took in the view of the entire lit-up Manhattan skyline from the back patio of Sin Carne. A prominent vegetarian city councilman proclaimed that Tyler's deconstructed pizza was the best slice in Brooklyn—heavy praise from a political heavyweight.

It was a good night for Noa, too. She worked the room, gliding, drink in hand, from group to group. A woman as beautiful as her feigning interest in other people always brings a smile to their faces. They were mesmerized by her. The animals were as good as saved, as far as Tyler was concerned.

He looked out from the kitchen and felt a sense of pride seeing Noa in a full charm offensive. He couldn't help but think, *I hit that*, as though he had heroically conquered some beautiful territory.

Tyler scanned the room and saw Damon powerwalking into the restaurant wearing an ultra-slim-cut gray tuxedo. He strolled into the kitchen like he owned the joint. There was no bro hug between them. Tyler debated telling him to get out, but he held his tongue.

"I don't mean to be a pain in the ass," Tyler said, "but the collection guy came by the other day. I thought you took care of that."

"I did. Did you drop my name?"

"No. I didn't want to—"

"Tyler, tell the guy to get fucked. Tell him you're Damon Fortunato's friend and I say you're off-limits. If me and you are gonna be in business together, I'm gonna need you to be a little more assertive, buddy," said Damon.

Tyler stood up a bit straighter.

"Look, I'm gonna mingle for a minute and grab a bite. I'll be back to shoot the shit with you. Looks like a great crowd."

"Thanks, man," Tyler said. "What brings you here anyway? Didn't figure you for the animal rights type."

"My wife thinks I came on account of her, but I'm here to keep an eye on you." Damon snaked out of the kitchen and disappeared into the crowd.

Tyler went back to work and heard a light knock on the kitchen door. It was Noa.

"Tyler," she said with her eyes still trained on the crowd. "Do you know who you were talking to?"

"That's that guy I was texting you about—the guy who wants to be my benefactor. I'll introduce you—he's probably a good guy to know."

"Yeah, sure," she said, voice trailing, "What does he do for a living?"

"Something to do with real estate and hospitality."

Noa laughed. "That's what he puts on his tax forms."

"I know what it looks like. But don't worry! I know how to take care of myself around guys like Damon Fortunato. I didn't fall off the turnip truck."

"Tyler," she said, "Damon Fortunato is my husband."

The color drained from Tyler's face. "You're kidding. Please tell me you're kidding . . ."

Her eyes looked glassy as they welled with tears, but none trickled down her cheek.

"Jesus Christ," Tyler said. "Greaser Jack's son is your fucking husband?"

"How did you meet him?" she asked him. Her hands were shaking.

"He came to the restaurant," Tyler said.

"When?" she asked.

Tyler took a second to think. "The day after I met you. He booked a late reservation last minute. We drank together. He wanted to help me franchise."

"Fuck," she said. "Tyler, he doesn't give a shit about plant-based cooking. This is bad."

"How bad?"

"You have to get the fuck out of here before he comes back. Where can you hide out?" she asked.

"I can't leave."

"Tyler!" She slapped him across the face. "This isn't a joke. You have to go NOW."

"An office. I have an office in the cellar," he said.

"Go there and stay there. I'll manage Damon up here. When the coast is clear, I'll come to get you," she said. "Go! Go now."

Tyler paused for a moment to see if she was serious. He saw the fear in her eyes, and he removed his apron. He did some deep breathing as he began to peel off his black latex gloves.

"Leave the gloves on," she said.

"Huh?"

"Just go. Go!" she said.

Tyler burst through the kitchen door and retreated when he saw Damon approaching. He ran around the kitchen in a panic before ducking under a counter to hide. He heard Damon and Noa talking: Damon asked if she'd seen the chef. She said she hadn't.

Damon said, "Great guy, that Tyler. I'd introduce you, but you met him already, right? The night you came home drunk and late, smelling like a whore."

"Why do you always do this?" she said.

"Do what, honey? What am I doing to you?"

Tyler heard sobbing.

"That's right, honey, nothing. Yet."

Damon pushed Noa through the door and back into the kitchen. He lifted her onto a counter and began to kiss her.

"Stop it," she said. "Someone might see us. These are my colleagues. Don't embarrass me in front of them."

"I wouldn't want to shame you in front of a bunch of crazy cat ladies. I gotta split and take care of something real quick anyway. Don't go anywhere."

Damon left her sitting on the counter. After counting to 25, Tyler emerged from his hiding spot and confronted Noa. "What the fuck is going on?"

"He's leaving, but you should still go to your office. I'll see you down there."

Tyler was angry, scared, confused—overwhelmed by a host of feelings he found uncomfortable. He marched out of the kitchen and ignored the crowd on his way to the basement. He turned on the office light and looked around for something he could use as a weapon. The best he could do was a wine bottle.

Noa knocked at the door and Tyler let her in.

"Where are the gloves?" she asked.

"Just how dangerous is this guy?"

She didn't answer and placed her pointer finger vertically over his lips to shush him.

"I have a thing for black latex gloves. Or nitrile. You know, people have allergies or whatever. It's like a fetish. I'm into some weird shit." Her hands moved down and she loosened his belt buckle.

"Are you out of your fucking mind?" he said.

"Fear is a turn-on. Don't act like it isn't. Your dick is rock hard."

She dropped to her knees and started with long, slow licks. When Noa took him all the way in, he lost all sense of time and place. He wrapped her hair around his fist and pulled her up for a passionate kiss. He pulled her gown above her hips and moved her thong to the side. Tyler took her from behind and she moaned as they fucked. They knocked over furniture and stacked boxes in his office. When he looked up to catch his breath, his eyes locked on Damon. Sitting in his office. He was filming them with his cell phone.

Tyler leapt off of Noa. He put one hand in front of his cock, still slick with the juices of Damon's wife.

"Mr. Fortunato, I can explain. When I met her, I had no idea she was your wife."

Noa stepped forward and placed her finger over Tyler's lips to shut him up again.

"You'll have a lot of explaining to do soon," said Damon.

"I told you, I didn't—"

Damon interrupted. "Not about Noa. I'm aware of what's going on there. I just don't know how you're going to explain the dead body in your dumpster."

"What?"

"Guy's name is Matteo," Damon said. "He was Noa's friend back in Providence. Good friend of hers, kinda like you. I drove that stiff down from Rhode Island in my trunk. He's getting ripe out there in your garbage. Now he's your problem. You're scheduled for the commercial waste carters tomorrow."

Noa grabbed Damon by the crotch as though she owned it and him along with it. "You take such good care of me," she said.

"I'm so hot right now. I'd do anything if you let me have you."

"Anything?" Noa asked.

Damon handed Noa the cell phone and she continued filming

"Why are you doing this?" Tyler shrieked with tears in his eyes.

"For the same reason you did. What any man would do," Damon said. "For her."

"He likes to watch and so do I," Noa said.

"Watch what?" Tyler asked, his hands shaking.

"The part that comes next," Noa said. She handed Damon a wood-handled hammer.

Damon stood up.

"I lied, Tyler. You won't need to explain anything to anyone," he said.

❖

Ben ordered an IPA for himself and a Chivas neat for the busty redhead seated next to him at the bar. She reminded him of a modern-day Joan Harris from *Mad Men*—she vibrated with sex appeal. He'd buy a woman like this as many drinks as it took to hold her attention.

"So, are you a local?" he asked.

"Oh, we just moved to Austin," she said.

"For work? Tech?"

"No," Noa said. "We needed a change of pace. There was this restaurant thing back in New York that didn't end up working out." She sipped her drink.

"Who's we? You got a boyfriend?"

"Husband, actually," she said. "But no worries. It's an unconventional relationship."

Herbert Johnson, ~1913

"Here it is: the sales pitch."

A Life of Idle Pleasure

Andrew Rucker Jones

M ornings are the worst. You'd think they would be great: you can sleep in, take your time, do anything you want. But trust me.

I look at the clock on my nightstand for the seventh time, its red digits pale in the direct sunlight. I stopped setting it months ago. We've had a blackout and the switch to daylight savings time since, but I think it's no more than a couple of hours off, so it could be time for a late brunch or a late lunch. Either way, late.

Nature calls. I toss the covers off my body, ten pounds heavier than it used to be despite muscle atrophy, and haul myself to a sitting position. I stand, sigh, smell my day-old-cat-toilet breath, and wander to the bathroom. I leave the door wide open—I live alone. It's not that there isn't a long list of women wanting to snag me or friends wanting to "pool our resources" and save on rent, but both ruses are obvious.

Done with the toilet, I step into the shower. Not for the world. For me. There was a time when I stopped bathing to see how people would react. I guess I should have known physical disgust sits deeper in the human psyche than greed. I had my bedsheets changed daily but still hardly found myself bearable.

As I stand under the hot water, I hear my father's voice in my head yelling at me to stop wasting water and electricity. I stick my tongue out at the wall and turn the hot water up to the far side of comforting but the near side of scalding. I hurry in spite of my spite.

After drying off, I don a new, still-fluffy bathrobe and pink slippers sporting huge alien heads over the toes—wide eyes, long proboscis, floppy ears. I think they're supposed to be elephant heads. I hope whoever was paid to design them wasn't paid much. Do they outsource design jobs like that to poor, underage kids in India? If not, it's about time.

In the kitchen, I check my voicemail while my bread toasts. Fifty-seven messages, the counter says. I delete them all. Only morbid curiosity makes me check. Anyone who wants to talk to me can come over.

I hit the depressor on the four-slice toaster upward to eject my single slice. I have the toaster turned all the way to "charcoal," then try to gauge when the toast is done by feel alone. It's a hobby. My toast comes up mottled black. I find a hint of ash adds character to my breakfast. If I can smell the ash, it's too much.

The butter hasn't had enough time to soften, so it clumps as I spread it on my warm toast. I take a bite where the butter is thickest and let the crumbs fall to the floor. The way I figure it, the maid has to vacuum anyway, so I'm doing her a favor by not making her wash another plate for my toast as well. These poor people have enough to do with their six children apiece, elderly parents, and three jobs each. I don't want to make that worse.

I eat my toast in disinterested nibbles and stare out the open window at the park two floors down. Kids screech in play. It's a school day, so they're small. The adults are employees: local daycare (Chinese), preschool (Vietnamese, and yes, I can usually tell the difference), a couple of roly-poly Hispanic sitters, and one hot Bolivian au pair. The one mother watching her son from a bench looks out of place. Don't blame me; I'm not racist. I'm just reporting how it is.

The informal, mid-day assembly in the park is completed by a man in his twenties sitting in full lotus position with a shaved head, light robes, and bells on his big toes. He wears a beatific smile as he chants the Hare Krishna Mahamantra and brushes hand cymbals together: closed, closed, open; *shk, shk, shing*. When someone drops a coin on the homespun cloth before him, he bows with his forehead to the ground without interrupting his mantra. I figure he goes back to his parents' condo at nightfall.

I'm done eating my toast, but I still stare at the dark-skinned, dark-haired au pair. It's a hobby. I know she's Bolivian because I overheard our doorman Jeremy talking her up, to which she responded in polite bewilderment. Jeremy made me sick and jealous at the same time. The au pair has an innocent, ancient-world, girl-next-door quality in the way she smiles, plays with the children like she's one of them, and brushes back her long hair from her face. The buoyancy of youth suffuses her motions, and she almost makes me think she enjoys her work.

She looks at the slender wristwatch on her delicate wrist and collects her two wards. They head down the street. The desire to engineer a run-in with her sparks something in me, but it passes. I can't imagine anything good coming of it.

I wonder about dinner. It's the next thing I have to look forward to. I thought of hiring a cook or maybe expanding the maid's duties, but the effort would be wasted on me. I'm no Epicurean. I find the possibilities inherent in bread, noodles, prepackaged spreads, cold cuts, sauces, and other accoutrements nearly limitless.

The buzzer plays "Dixie," answering the question of what to do next. The buzzer is a holdover from my infatuation with *The Dukes of Hazzard* when I was a kid. Boss Hog was my favorite. He was so smarmy and opulent in that pristine white suit and hat. I figured if it weren't for the Dukes, he could get away with plenty of scintillating petty malfeasance. That would have made a better story.

I shamble over to the intercom. "Who is it, Jeeves?"

The doorman sounds as tired of my joke as I am, but I still don't give it up. It's a hobby. "It's *Jeremy*, Luke."

"I don't know a Jeremy. Don't let him in."

"You know what I mean, Luke."

"Fine," I say. "So who is it?"

"It's your good twin."

"I don't have a twin, good or evil. Who is it?"

"Luke."

"What?"

"Luke! It's Luke, Luke!"

"Oh. Oh, I get it now. Yeah, okay. Let him in, I guess." I click off and look through the doorless archway to the living room where a full-length mirror hangs. I lift a hand to push my damp hair into a rough part but let my hand drop again. Screw it.

I peer through the peephole in the door. After a while, Luke walks into view. He knocks with the perfect balance of ambitious expectation and demure obeisance. He's wearing business casual, not too formal for meeting an old friend, but groomed enough to convince. He holds something small and wrapped. He fidgets a little and knocks again. He wants something. I sigh, roll my eyes, and open the door.

"Luke," I greet him with the aspect of a dead fish.

"Luke," he responds with a blitz appraisal of my person, head to foot. We were childhood friends, both born into religious families: his Christianity, mine space opera. "You look well," he lies. "Very relaxed." He sneaks another look at my alien slippers and Legend of Zelda bathrobe. I know he's wondering if I'm naked underneath. I am.

"How's life treating you, Luke?" I walk ahead of him into the living room and indicate a low, overstuffed chair. I sit at the near end of the matching couch.

"Fine, thank you. I don't have to ask how life is treating you, do I?" He chuckles and I sport a tight smile. "Nice place."

"It was my one indulgence when I won the lottery."

"That and quitting your job, I hear."

"That's less an indulgence than a logical step. Isn't that what every lottery winner does?"

"I suppose. I haven't done the research. Here, I've brought you a present." Luke half-stands again to hand me the gift. I don't budge as I take it. When I shake it, it makes no sound.

"I'm pretty sure I already have one of these. Or I don't want one."

"I'm certain you don't and you do. Open it!"

I remove the tape piece by piece. Luke's legs are crossed, and I can see his impatience in the wiggle of his free foot. I smirk to myself.

After removing the last strip of tape, I place the wrapping paper beside me on the couch. "It's a book. You might not believe it, but I do have a couple of these, and I really didn't want another."

"It's not just any book." Luke jumps forward to snatch it, turn it spine up, and replace it in my hands. "It's a book on e-paper." There is a tiny socket at the base of the spine.

To kill time, I feign mild interest. "E-paper, huh? Never heard of it."

"It's a prototype," Luke begins in a rush, "but it works in field tests. I've been using one for two weeks."

Here it is: the sales pitch.

"E-paper was developed a while ago, but it's just now becoming market-ready. In a nutshell, it's enhanced paper with an encapsulated layer of ink pressed to both sides. By applying an electric charge, the ink can be reconfigured. We can reprint the book in your hand to be any book you want. Just hook it up to a computer equipped with our software and upload."

Behind his grin, Luke's teeth seem whiter and straighter than I remember. I raise my eyebrows without widening my eyes and my head bobs like a buoy on a calm sea. It's the most enthusiasm I can muster.

"That's nice, Luke, but why do I need it? I'm not much of a reader, you know." This is true, but it's also exactly the lead I know he's hoping for. It's a game, and playing it keeps me occupied.

"It's the thought that counts, right? This thought is a business opportunity." Luke is effervescent. I hate it when they get this way, but it's unavoidable. He delivered the hook, and now he thinks he has my interest, so he settles in for his full spiel.

"Our market research proves there's a significant market for e-paper. Young people never touch printed materials, and old people will take traditional paper books with them to the grave, but there is a generation in between that knows its habits are anachronistic, but is convinced it *needs* the feel of a book in the hand. They're nostalgic and cling to the haptic connection, but they also grasp the benefits of e-books. *This—*" Luke points at the object in my lap, "—is for them."

Next, I'm supposed to ask reasonable but skeptical questions. "That's a pretty thin market segment, isn't it? Those people won't be around for long."

Luke waves the problem away. "A decade, maybe longer, but that doesn't matter. Once the market dwindles, we segue into something related, find a partner, or outright sell to the highest bidder and walk away with the cash. Not every business opportunity lasts for generations. Take what you find and run with it."

I run my fingertips across the smooth cover, which, at the moment, bears the title *Moby Dick, Part I*, then stop with my fingers cupped as if around a baseball and tap the cover once. "And you think people will go in for this? If they change their reading habits, why wouldn't they switch all the way? I see it as an all-or-nothing proposition."

"Oh, we know there are people out there who love this idea. Think of it this way: when you learn to ride a bike, do you jump on and start riding? No. You start with training wheels. These are training wheels for e-books."

"When you say it *that* way . . ." This, I learned, is a magical phrase for entrepreneurs. I love to dangle it in front of them and watch them beg.

Luke leans forward into hope. His sculpted, blond hair bobs, and his blue eyes erupt in a cold fire of imagined shared understanding. "Yes, training wheels! What's more, once the ink is configured, e-paper doesn't need electricity. You can take this baby on a trip to Australia and never worry about your battery dying."

I widen my eyes and keep the sarcasm out of my voice. "Now *that's* an advantage."

"You bet it is. We should discuss the possibilities at length over dinner tonight."

There's the invitation. I refrain from rubbing my hands and cackling. "With me? It's a nice gift, and it would be great to catch up over dinner, but what do I have to do with your business plan?"

This part always makes them uncomfortable. No one likes begging. "Well, Luke, we have a great idea, a prototype, solid market research, and we're building marketing channels, but there are a few more technical details we have to hammer out, and then we have to go into mass production. The whole venture has been a little more expensive than we initially calculated. I was hoping you might invest to help get this beauty to market."

I purse my lips and cross my arms. They don't believe it if they don't have to work for it, and it's no fun if they don't believe it.

Luke rushes into the breach. "Hey, if I were to tell you it's a sure thing, I would be lying. Nothing in life is a sure thing. But if we can pull this off—and we're close—we'll make a bundle. And this time when I say 'we,' I include you." Luke clasps his hands in front of him and leans so far forward I hope he tips. "You see, Luke, we're not asking for a loan. We're asking you to be an angel investor. Yeah, if we fail, you lose your investment, but if we *succeed*, Luke, if we succeed, you'll rake in the dough!"

"Rake in the dough, you say?" I stroke my chin, stubbly since I last shaved two days ago. "We are talking about money and not baked goods, correct?"

Luke rolls his eyes. "What do you say, Luke? Are you in?"

I continue to stroke my chin as if in thought. I even tug my earlobe once, something I've never tried before. It seems to heighten Luke's tension. I resolve to try it again the next chance I get. After a last caress of my finger down the spine of the e-paper book in my lap, I look at Luke and harrumph loud enough for the neighbors to hear. Luke startles easily.

"Not a chance. But if you still want to take me out to dinner, I'd love to." I smile like the Hare Krishna in the park.

"What? You're really not interested?" Luke's mouth hangs open at my bluntness. I'm used to it. "If you're worried about losing your investment, I'll create an oversight position for you in the company so you have your finger on our pulse."

"Posh, Luke, I'm not worried—wait . . . are you . . . offering me a job?"

A smile spreads across his face. "Sure, buddy! Hey, do you remember that business we started together in fourth grade?"

"The shoelace thing . . ."

"L Squared's Secondhand Shoelace Shop!"

"Your mom thought it was 'unchristian' to buy the extra shoelace off kids when one in a pair broke, then sell it back to them for more."

Luke waves a hand. "My mother doesn't understand value creation. First, we bought laces for a penny more than our customers could get from the trash can. Second, everybody knew they could buy laces cheap from us."

"Two cents per lace, five for a matching pair—supplies limited."

"That was the value we created: people knew where to buy and sell used laces, and we were cheaper than the competition."

I'm quiet a moment, remembering when his mother made us throw our entire inventory away—ten laces, two of which were a matching pair. "Didn't do us much good."

Luke raises an eyebrow. "We earned enough to buy an ice cream cone each. Isn't that something? Hey, buddy." He leans in and puts a hand on my knee. "We had fun. We did good. And we could do that again. I remember you had a head for numbers. My company could use that."

Children's voices from the sidewalk outside my window remind me of the au pair. "Could I hire my own secretary?"

Luke smirks. "Depends on how much you invest. You in?"

The buzzer plays "Dixie" again, and I shamble to the door. It's my maid Martina, who smiles even while she cleans the toilet. She bustles in, places my newspaper on the couch, and grabs a rag from the broom closet in one practiced movement. Seeing that I have company, she nods and smiles at Luke and hurries off to the master bathroom to start her chores. Too bad I haven't brushed my teeth yet today. Now the glob of toothpaste will hang in the sink until Martina comes back tomorrow.

I shamble back over to the couch where Luke is waiting.

"Well? Are you in?"

I should be thinking about e-paper and numbers and a Bolivian secretary, but all I can think about is toothpaste stuck in the sink—blue-and-white and drying. Bile rises in my throat.

"Not a chance, my friend. Count me out." It comes out with more force behind it than I intend. I realize I'm angry for the first time in months. "In fact, do yourself a favor and count yourself out. I don't want you to head down this path, Luke. There's nothing there but hard, bitter work. Let it go and live a little."

Luke leans back and stares at me. "Look, pal, some of us actually have to work for a living."

"But not like this." I get up and pace in front of the couch. "Get a job behind a counter, or tend someone's garden. Walk dogs. Hammer nails. Wax floors." I stop in front of him. "Do something you don't care about. Pay the bills with as little lifeblood as possible. With the rest of your time, enjoy yourself!"

"That's a nice thought, but I have a wife and baby. We need more than I can earn waxing floors. Invest in my business, and I can provide for them."

I'm agitated at this point and run my hand through my hair. How can I sell him on this? "I'll do you one better. Most of my visitors are gold diggers. Way back when we knew each other, and maybe they would succeed with whatever cockamamie business ventures they peddle, but they don't care about me, and I don't care about them.

You're different. We only see each other a couple times a year, but you're my friend."

"Some way to treat a friend, leading me on like that," Luke says.

"Just listen. For you and you alone, I'm willing to offer a life of idle pleasure like mine. I would fund you at your current standard of living for the rest of your life—you and your wife and whatever children you have—if you'll give up this business venture, kick your heels up, and take life easy."

Luke arches an eyebrow. "You want to pay for my entire family? You want to put my kid through college?"

"Yes! I want you to give up work and relax with them. Take them to see the world. Watch your child grow. Spoil your wife with attention. Just don't run yourself into the ground chasing after the pot of gold at the end of the rainbow." I sit back down, my fury spent but eager for his answer. "Please, Luke. Be good to yourself."

He strokes his chin and thinks for a while. He tugs at his earlobe once. "You drive a hard bargain," he says, "but no."

I'm flabbergasted, and I don't use that word often. "No? You would turn down an offer like that?"

"I would and I am." Luke's body is relaxed, his expression flat.

I want to say something witty, but all that comes out is, "Why?"

He picks up the book and opens it flat on one hand. He holds a single leaf with the other, its thin edge facing me. "This is 105.35 grams per square millimeter, the same thickness as résumé paper. It took five Ph.Ds. forty-eight trials over thirteen months to get it that thin, and I personally visited twenty-five banks to fund the R&D overruns. This device—" he snaps it shut in my face, "—has no battery. It can't generate an electrical current. My engineers and my wife say I'm nuts, but when I turn the lights off at night, I can hear it hum on my nightstand. It calms me to sleep and wakes me in the morning. That's why."

Martina hurries through the room as I put Luke's gift to my ear, then she hurries back again with a vacuum cleaner in her hands.

Luke waves at her. "Hola señora. ¿Cómo estás?"

Her smile deepens the crow's feet at her eyes. "Muy bien gracias, señor," and she's gone around the corner into my room where the vacuum cleaner whines to life and crumbs ricochet inside the hose. The hose is attached to a floor unit on casters, which don't roll well on the thick carpeting. I've been thinking about getting one of those vacuuming robots so she doesn't have to work as much. I could pay her less, which is a nice bonus.

"I wish you would reconsider my proposal," Luke says and pulls a business card out of his breast pocket where he must have had it waiting for this moment, though I'm sure he didn't imagine the conversation ending this way. He places it on the armrest of his chair.

I slouch deeper into the couch and shrug in return. "If your answer stays no, my answer stays no. But I just don't understand you."

"Nor I you, old friend. Winning the lottery gave you so many possibilities—"

"—Which I take advantage of daily. I don't have to work for the rest of my life, Luke. It's a dream come true." I maintain eye contact, but if truth be told, I'm growing bored of this, and I feel sleep preying on me.

Luke walks to the door but glances at the business card on the armrest, probably wondering if Martina will throw it away. She might. I'm leaving it to chance.

"Well, Luke," he says, "even if we don't see eye to eye on this, it's been a pleasure. We haven't talked in a while. We could still go out to dinner, you know . . . if you're free."

I open the door for him. "That depends on how many more old friends hit me up for money today. Turning down freeloaders is a time-consuming hobby."

"Call me if you change your mind, and think about a change of clothes."

"Zelda is a classic."

The sound of children barreling down the hallway makes me look out. The Bolivian au pair herds the two children in her care past me. They have a doughnut each in their hands. I watch her as she passes, and I think I smell rainforest, though I have no idea what rainforest smells like. She looks at me and smiles such an innocent smile that my heart flips. I don't know if they have The Legend of Zelda or aliens in Bolivia, but I'm glad she doesn't look below my face. I continue to stare as she unlocks the condominium across the hall and down one, then herds the children inside. She really *is* the girl next door. She casts a glance in my direction, and I think I see her smile when she discovers me gawking. She ducks inside and closes the door.

"Strike that, Luke. I have an engagement for this evening. You enjoy your time with your family."

"Then I'll do that, but—" he pokes a finger in my face, "—think about it." He swaggers out the door. Except for the swagger and a few other things, Jeremy was onto something: he does kind of look like my distant twin. Or I look like his distant twin. I wonder briefly what a "distant twin" is.

"Think about what?" I call after Luke, but I'm looking the other way, toward where the au pair lives. "The business deal or dinner?"

"Both," he replies.

"Does Bolivia have a rainforest?" I yell after him, but he's gone. I wait for a second longer to see if the au pair will reemerge to answer my question as an expert on Bolivia, but the hallway remains empty. I close my door.

I stand for a moment with my back to the door. Martina has moved on to the living room. I watch her push and pull the vacuum cleaner tube in rapid strokes, jerking the base behind her every few strokes. It's mesmerizing but unsettling. I tear myself away and lift the newspaper off the couch. I scan the headlines as I walk toward my bedroom to put some clothes on but stop in front of the kitchen. *Why bother?* I think, and toss the newspaper in the recycling bin. I've been meaning to cancel that subscription for a while.

I halt again on the threshold of my bedroom. There was something I wanted to do, something I wanted to get dressed for. Oh, yeah. The hot Bolivian. I consider for a moment. Shrugging to myself, I give in; it's probably not worth it. I close the door behind me, flop onto my bed, and kick my alien slippers off. The muted *shk, shk, shing* from the park exerts a soporific effect on me. I close my eyes and cocoon into the sheets Martina just made—firm enough to bounce a quarter off of.

"Failing to reach an agreeable resolution, the client contacted VanGuard to employ us to settle the matter in her favor."

Invasive Species

Sam Wiebe

This document is to be viewed by Mrs. Doncaster or her legal representative and no one else. It is not to be removed from the offices of VanGuard Solutions. Once payment is received on all outstanding invoices, the document and attachments will be deleted, the device it was composed on demagnetized and destroyed. Only a record of the transaction will be retained, for tax purposes.

Initial Consultation

On 4/3/23, Mrs. Doncaster (hereafter 'THE CLIENT') met with Mr. Gadd and myself to discuss a matter pertaining to her neighbor, Mr. Robert Lamb. The client at first sought remedy directly from Mr. Lamb. Financial inducements, threats of legal action, and appeals to community spirit failed to move Mr. Lamb towards the client's position. Failing to reach an agreeable resolution, the client contacted VanGuard to employ us to settle the matter in her favor.

Over the following work day, Mr. Gadd and I developed an actionable seven-point plan, along with an estimated fee for its successful execution. Both were agreed to in writing by the client. Upon receipt of a deposit, Mr. Gadd and I set to work.

Step One: Assessment

Robert Anton Lamb is 47, married to Elsa Nemeth Lamb, 46. The Lambs have a son, Jeremy, 22, currently enrolled at Northside

Community College. The family owns the property at 22 Alma Lane, a two-story prefabricated house with unfenced front and back yards. They own a rescue collie named Chester.

While not strictly neighbors, Mr. Lamb's property is situated on a foothill below but in the line of sight from the client's summer estate. The two have maintained a polite but awkward acquaintance, in part stemming from the client's refusal to donate money to a charitable organization Mrs. Lamb solicits for. Mr. Gadd insisted the client not vary her social interactions with the Lambs, as this might tip them off to her involvement.

Mr. Lamb has been employed by the Big Val You grocery chain for seventeen years. He is currently the Senior Produce Manager, overseeing the fruit and vegetable purchases for all six outlets. He earns $71,456 annually, including matching 401K contributions and the 'silver' tier of the Big Val You employee dental plan. Mrs. Lamb, a substitute teacher, earns on average $34,000. The Lambs lease a 2016 Yukon and have no outstanding debts.

Both Mr. and Mrs. Lamb attend the Northside Unitarian Church infrequently. They have sex infrequently. Both seem monogamous and relatively content.

Mr. Lamb is an avid gardener who chairs the local chapter of the Green Thumb Society. Community opinion is that he is a conscientious, reliable, and unexciting person.

Step Two: Preparation

Three cameras were installed behind the Lamb property. Care was taken that Mr. Lamb's cluster of oak and apple trees ('the orchard') did not impede sightlines into the house. Around-the-clock surveillance was considered, but deemed unnecessary, as our goal is inductive.

Mr. Gadd spent three days researching horticulture, while I gained a passing familiarity with the neighborhood bars around Northside Community College. VanGuard agents observed Mrs. Lamb's monthly meeting of the Northside Book Club, as well as a series of pool games (nine ball) between Mr. Lamb and a work colleague. Mr. Lamb was not the victor.

Step Three: Insinuation

The Green Thumb Society has a new member: Gene Pruitt, 40, a biochemist renting a property at 34 Allegra Drive. Pruitt's gardening materials are in transit from his home in Bristol, and while he has no garden to speak of, he is a willing volunteer who enjoys the social aspect of gardening clubs. In his spare time he writes papers on the health of forests for an obscure horticultural society in Britain.

Over coffee, Mr. Lamb and Mr. Pruitt remarked upon several similarities in their interests and philosophical outlooks, including a shared enjoyment of what Mr. Pruitt calls "billiards." They played two games, Mr. Lamb winning both. Mr. Pruitt met also Mrs. Lamb briefly when she came to pick up her husband. The two chatted about a recent bestseller both had read. Both found the book's plot contrived and uninspiring.

Meanwhile, Jeremy Lamb has begun a friendship with Dana Sanders, a student who frequents the Book N Brew Pub. Ms. Sanders, 26, was asked out by Jeremy, and after some hesitation, agreed.

At the end of their meal (French fries, chicken fingers, ten Miller High Lifes), Ms. Sanders insisted on paying the bill using her student meal card. The Book N Brew is the only establishment on campus which allows alcoholic beverages to be purchased using these cards.

The two returned to Jeremy's dormitory. Some light kissing and inexpert groping occurred, over the course of which, Ms. Sanders confessed that she has a friend in the Student Union who tops up her meal card account without her having to deposit money. Some discussion of the ethics of this followed. Jeremy came around to the viewpoint that it was 'a victimless crime,' and Ms. Sanders agreed to 'hook him up.'

All in all, Mr. Gadd's establishment as Gene Pruitt and my own as Dana Sanders was highly successful.

Step Four: Symptoms

At the 5/14/23 meeting of the Green Thumb Society, a fine grey particulate was observed on cuttings brought in by Mr. Lamb from his dwarf apple. Mr. Lamb expressed surprise, and insisted that when he took the cuttings the previous evening, they "looked A-OK" to him. Mr. Pruitt asked if he could take one of these cuttings for study; he has relevant literature at home, and could provide a better idea of the powder's origin.

Later that day, Mr. Pruitt met with Mrs. Lamb at a coffee shop to borrow her copy of next month's book club selection, a regency romance. Mrs. Lamb warned him the book was a "cheesy potboiler" with little to recommend it. Mr. Pruitt brought her flowers as a reciprocal gift, and insisted on paying for her coffee.

At the college, Dana Sanders has taken Jeremy Lamb out for drinks four times this week, resulting in Jeremy's first missed assignment. All four have been at the Book N Brew, and were charged to Jeremy's meal card. In lieu of romance, a friendship has formed between them, based on their shared affinity for alcohol. Ms. Sanders confessed to being impressed by "a man who can really hold his booze." After last call on 5/16/23, a conversation between them turned to whether Jeremy was "really and truly meant" for post-secondary education.

Late at night on 5/17/23, Mr. Pruitt interrupted the Lamb family at their home. The grey particulate, he warned, was a blight connected to a rare Dutch Breeder moth which feasts on the bark of *malus domesticus*. An infestation could have dire results for local flora and fauna. Mr. Pruitt inquired as to whether Mr. Lamb observed any moth cocoons or insect carcasses in his orchard. A negative answer was given.

Mr. Pruitt explained that containment of the moth was a priority. Citing relevant literature, he showed the Lambs that the most prudent option would be to dispose of any trees showing signs of infestation. Failure to do so, Mr. Pruitt argued, would be catastrophic. Mr. Lamb once again stated he had seen no sign of the moths, and was not going to destroy his orchard "on a goddamn whim."

Mr. Pruitt insisted that any findings should be reported to the Green Thumb Society immediately. Mr. Lamb agreed, on the condition Mr. Pruitt left the property and allow them to go back to sleep.

At 0437 hours the morning of 5/18/23, Camera B captured Mr. Lamb in his pajamas and slippers inspecting his orchard. Mr. Lamb made note of more gray particulate. After checking the trees with a flashlight and stepladder, he retrieved the three dead moth specimens our agent secreted. Camera A captured Mr. Lamb disposing of these in his downstairs toilet.

Step Five: Escalation

Mr. Lamb met with the president of Big Val You on 5/19/23. Over the weekend several moths were observed in the produce section of the Northside store. When one flew out of Mr. Lamb's car at lunchtime, a coworker alerted the president. No immediate action was taken and the event was attributed to coincidence.

A warm friendship continues to grow between Mr. Pruitt and Mrs. Lamb. When the latter isn't substituting at a school, they have a standing appointment for "coffee and book talk" at a local café. Mr. Pruitt is an affectionate person—hugs, cheek kisses and frequent pats on the hand and shoulder are frequently observed by other patrons.

On 5/21/23, Mrs. Lamb confessed that her husband did in fact find insect remains in his orchard, disposing of them rather than alerting the Society as promised. She explained that Mr. Lamb had planted many of those trees himself and "would just die" if any harm happened to them.

Mrs. Lamb's tearful confession caused Mr. Pruitt great alarm. She elicited from him a promise not to tell her husband that she had told him. Agitated but honorable to the last, Mr. Pruitt agreed.

At Ms. Sanders's urging, Jeremy Lamb has withdrawn from his Geography and Statistics classes. He has a growing reputation for imbibing copious amounts of liquor, and is affectionately referred to as "Tank." Two friends of Jeremy's have also begun drinking using the meal card, paying Jeremy a small fee for every round ordered.

On 5/23/23, Jeremy and one of these friends were cited for public mischief, and on 5/25/23, Jeremy received a DUI. He mentioned neither occurrence to his parents at the family's Sunday dinner.

Step Six: Crescendo

At the 5/29/23 meeting of the Green Thumb Society, several members testified to finding grey particulate in their gardens. One had video evidence of moths, which Mr. Pruitt confirmed as the Dutch Breeder variety.

After Mr. Lamb's protestations and insistence on calm, Mr. Pruitt took the floor. Unable to hold his piece given the gravity of the situation, he related his conversation with Mrs. Lamb about her husband's findings and deception. An accusation of an affair was thrown back at Pruitt, who denied it, though not vociferously.

Forestry experts were called. The following Tuesday, twelve Dutch Breeder moths were removed from Mr. Lamb's dwarf apple.

A word-of-mouth campaign, along with some judicious postering (see attached 'STOP THE SPREAD' flyer design) continued over the following week. Facing a public relations crisis, on 6/3/23, Big Val You placed Mr. Lamb on indefinite unpaid leave.

After a public incident involving the Dean of Admission's vehicle, Jeremy Lamb's deception with the student meal card system was discovered. Choosing to protect Ms. Sanders, he admitted to planning and carrying out the scam on his own. He is currently awaiting expulsion.

Step Seven: Harvest

After Mr. Lamb's suicide on 6/7/23, the property at Alma Street was placed on the market. With Mr. Lamb's consent and the Forestry department's insistence, the orchard and garden were razed and replaced with a stylish concrete patio extension.

Elsa Lamb has decided to return to her maiden name of Cross. She desires to sell the house quickly and return to her hometown of Chillicothe. She is no longer a member of the Northside Book Club.

Jeremy Lamb waited until after the funeral to tell his mother about his expulsion, presenting this as a cry for independence. He has moved out of student housing into a shared basement flat with three roommates. He is currently employed as a Submarine Sandwich Artist.

The release of Dutch Breeder moths has led several members of the Green Thumb Society, including its interim chairperson, to give up horticultural pursuits entirely. As anticipated, damage to local flora and fauna has been extensive (see attached tables and map). Specimens have been observed as far as one hundred miles to the south, and may have crossed the state lines.

The desired result has thus been achieved: the oak trees which impeded Mrs. Doncaster's view from her summer estate are no more. Mr. Gadd and I are confident whoever buys the Lamb property will not attempt to grow anything as large and offensive to the eye.

Our invoice is attached. We appreciate prompt payment. Thank you so much for choosing VanGuard Solutions.

"'Cool.' He kept his arms at his side. 'Sayin' I saw some fucked-up shit in one of the houses I'm workin' at, would ya'll wanna know?'"

The Old Money Beat

Curtis Ippolito

On the Thursday of my first week as a reporter, the newspaper's publisher, Arch Winston, called me to his office from over the loudspeaker.

A chorus of chiding *ooooos* floated above the cubicle farm. I jumped to my feet, swept the hair out of my eyes, and hustled to the elevator. I'd never met the man, yet his presence loomed large among the rank and file. The only way I knew what he looked like that first week was thanks to a gaudy painting of him that hung above the copier.

I punched the fifth-floor button and the elevator rose with a jerk. *Park Cities News* occupied the first floor of the building, while Arch's primary media ambition, *Metroplex Magazine*, maintained offices on the entire third and fourth floors. He, his wife, Carol, and *Metroplex Magazine*'s managing editor had the fifth floor to themselves. Word was, Arch bought our neighborhood newspaper—which covered Highland Park and University Park, two of the richest neighborhoods in Dallas referred to in tandem as the Park Cites—so he could give readers the hard-hitting news they expected from the major daily paper, but with a touch of class the area was accustomed to. So far, I'd reported on a rash of stolen copper gutters—two whole incidents—a bakery opening specializing in petit fours, and had been put in charge of the calendar of community events.

The fifth floor was cold. Arch's office had his name and "Publisher and Chief" etched on the double glass doors. He saw me, and waved me in.

"Oliver. Thank you for joining us." Arch stayed lounged in his high-back white leather chair. He wore a shiny Navy-blue suit and red tie, accented with gold cufflinks and gold watch. His hair was slicked back with a shock of silver at his temples and his face appeared unnaturally tan for the season: a dead-ringer for the painting downstairs. My managing editor, Cliff, occupied one of the two chairs opposite Arch. On the white leather couch to the right sat a woman about Arch's age in a black dress. Her legs were crossed at the ankles.

"It's nice to meet you, sir." I offered my hand across the desk. He made minimal effort to cross the divide, but did shake my hand. "Hi, Cliff," I said. He nodded.

"Take a seat, Oliver," Arch said. "I have some good news for you."

"Sure thing." I sat and quickly scanned the room. Dark wood artifacts and art of African heritage lined glass shelving on either wall. Specialized lights showcased each piece. Pottery, tools, weapons, carvings, and masks. I didn't know shit about art, but it made a statement.

"Cliff tells me you're fitting in downstairs and taking everything he assigns you."

I nodded.

"He's a go-getter," Cliff said.

"Excellent to hear. Oliver, what I'm about to tell you is sensitive. First, let me say, and I think you'll agree, that we have an obligation as journalists to ensure we uncover ugliness and shine a light on injustice."

"Yes, of course, Mr. Winston."

"Call me Arch. Everyone does."

"Yes, sir."

"Oliver, meet my wife, Carol, over there." I leaned forward to make eye contact with the woman on the couch. Carol smiled. I waved. "A year ago, the manager at Carol's hair salon fondled her during her appointment."

"I'm so sorry to hear that," I said.

"Thank you." Arch continued. "She didn't tell me about it right away, and in fact, didn't report it in any way for several months. When she was mentally and emotionally prepared to do so, Dallas police told us the inappropriate behavior didn't rise to the level of sexual assault, so no charges could be filed."

My head was spinning with where this was going. I had questions, but Arch's presence made me feel like asking anything until he was done would be like interrupting Sunday Mass with a flash mob.

He leaned forward, planting his elbows on his mahogany desk. "Cliff is going to assign you this story for Saturday's paper. It's a tight turnaround, but Carol will provide you the rest of the background. Interview the manager, Kim Wong, and write it up with a headline to the effect of, 'Local salon manager accused of fondling Highland Park socialite.' Keep Carol's identity anonymous. Sound good?"

"You don't want me to explore why the police didn't charge him?" I asked.

Arch waved a hand. "No. Maybe for a follow-up piece. For now, focus on exposing this asshole's behavior. You do this correctly, and your story could help keep other women from experiencing the same trauma my wife has endured. That's why you became a reporter, right?"

I looked at Carol. Her head was bowed. Contemplative. "O—okay, Mr., uh, Arch."

"Perfect. Cliff, why don't we clear the room so Carol and Oliver can chat. I trust you have a notepad with you, Oliver?"

I raised and showed the one I'd been taking notes in the entire time.

❖

I interviewed Carol Winston for ten minutes. Her story was brief, the account not as detailed as I would have hoped. She said this Kim Wong fondled her breasts mid-shampoo. Her stylist had left her head reclined in the sink for her hair to drain while she ran to get supplies. Mr. Wong approached, groped her, and left. She said she was too shocked to scream or say anything, and it took her months to process the event, as Arch had said. Something seemed incomplete about the story, but I told myself to do the reporting and see what I could find out.

Besides, I was in no position to turn down assignments.

Twenty-four at the time, I'd graduated journalism school a year earlier. This being my first legit, full-time job in the newspaper business, I aimed to make a good impression through old-fashioned dedication and hard work. Same as the pavement-pounders and investigative rock stars I'd idolized since my high school newspaper days.

When I returned to the newsroom, several of my coworkers looked to be heading out.

"Grabbing lunch at Del's on the square," said Bruce, an older reporter with a hippie vibe. He wore one hoop earring and smoked Swisher Sweets. "Want to join us?"

"What's Del's? How much?"

"Burger place. C'mon, I'll cover you."

"Thanks. I can get you back next week."

"Tough waiting on that first check, huh?"

"No kidding." My first day, we all ate at Whole Foods. I got two slices of pizza, a side salad, and a fancy can of soda and spent eleven bucks. I'm just glad my debit card went through and I didn't have to put everything back.

We got to Del's in five minutes. It was beautiful outside for a January day. Clear, in the 60s. Knowing Dallas though, it'd be 25 and windy as hell tomorrow.

After ordering, we waited at our table. I took advantage of the downtime to query my colleagues about my new story assignment.

"I don't know," Bruce said, shrugging. "Sounds a little iffy, but if Arch wants you to do it, the man writes our checks."

"No harm in doing the reporting," said Julie. She was our assistant managing editor, even though she was only two years older than me. "Your job is to tell both sides of the issue and let the reader decide who's in the wrong, if anyone."

"Okay. I can do that."

Our food came and the conversation shifted to office politics and rumors. We were in a wage freeze, apparently. And the assistant ME before Julie had been fired after being caught having an affair with a member of the school board.

I got up to refill my Dr Pepper. While I was filling my cup, a Black guy my age wearing a reflective vest and work boots hovered.

"Ya'll reporters?" he finally asked.

I set my soda down, and flashed the press credential around my neck. I was still pretty excited to have one. "Yes. We're with *Park Cities News*. I'm Oliver."

"Cool." He kept his arms at his side. "Sayin' I saw some fucked-up shit in one of the houses I'm workin' at, would ya'll wanna know?"

"What kind of shit?"

"Nazi shit. Memorabilia and whatnot. A whole room of it."

I cringed. Nazi memorabilia? "Yes, potentially. If the owner's notable, that would definitely be news." It might be even if not. My mind raced.

"It's the Hunter mansion. I don't know the dude's first name. I'm just a grunt."

"Well, I'm new to the area. Hunter doesn't ring a bell." Truth told, the only Park Cities residents I knew by name so far were the owner of the Dallas Cowboys and a former Texas governor. "Did you take any photos?"

"With what? My flip phone?"

I shrugged.

The prospect of outing a rich, influential resident for owning Nazi artifacts sounded like a career-maker, but with nothing more than this guy's word, I didn't know how I could prove it. Not like the owner would fess up to even my toughest questioning. "That's messed up, but I need more. Are you done working there?"

He took a deep breath. His body language said he was done talking with me. Then, "Naw, we got two more days there. Rich fools havin' us rip out their brand-new kitchen cause black granite is out and marble is in, or some shit."

"If you can take pictures—maybe bring a disposable camera—and get them to me . . . In the meantime, I'll research who this guy is." I jotted down my desk phone number and the paper's address on a piece of paper, handed it to him. "Thanks for the heads-up."

"Sure."

Back at the table I asked if anyone knew who the Hunters were.

"As in Martin Hunter?" said Bruce. "He's only one of the richest Highland Park residents. Old money. His father was a shipping magnate. Martin went the real estate route. His influence spans the Park Cities and Dallas and is immense. If there's a major construction or redevelopment project going, Martin Hunter's likely involved."

"He is also a beloved philanthropist," chimed in Colette, our lifestyle/arts reporter who looked more like a college professor. "His gifts reinvigorated the arts scene in HP and Dallas."

"Why do you ask?" Bruce asked.

No way I wanted to let them in on what I had just been told after that glowing history lesson. "No reason. Just trying to learn people and names."

❖

When we got back to the newsroom, I hopped online to do research on Arch's story.

I found out the salon Kim Wong managed was part of a small chain, Fashion Styles, with locations in Cedar Springs, Uptown, and East Dallas. Wong worked at the Cedar Springs location. He had no priors, and no disciplinary action against his cosmetology license. I sent an email to the cosmetology board to confirm the latter. I sent another to corporate Fashion Styles, seeking comment on their policy pertaining to employees accused of sexual impropriety.

According to the county tax accessor, Wong owned a home in East Dallas. I scribbled down the address, along with a phone number listed for him.

With that, I left for the salon to conduct interviews.

Fashion Styles was a typical salon. A one-room establishment with sinks and styling stations. All the stylists were women, and Korean. I found it curious someone of Carol Winston's stature would go to a no-frills establishment in a not-affluent part of town. I figured rich women got their hair styled at Nordstrom's or high-end salons. But what did I know?

Mr. Wong wasn't working. Disappointing. But I did interview the four stylists working. Two said Mr. Wong was friendly and respectful. The other two didn't speak the best English, so I didn't get much from them.

Before driving back to the paper, I called Mr. Wong's number. It went to voicemail, but was his number. I asked him to call me back about a story I was working on, though I didn't describe what it was about. Didn't want to scare him off before I even started.

Back at the paper, no replies from the cosmetology board or corporate Fashion Styles. I opened a Word document, typed up the quotes from the two stylists, and Carol's quotes with "Highland Park socialite" as attribution. I leaned back. Computer keys tapped across the newsroom. The white noise aided my wandering mind. I hoped that construction worker would take pictures of what he'd seen. Shit, I didn't get his name. Rookie mistake. Even though Arch's story was due tomorrow, I figured some light research on Martin Hunter wouldn't hurt. But I didn't find any more online than my colleagues had already shared with me.

Next, I swung by our archive wall, which stored the previous 12 months of papers on-hand, and found Martin and his wife, Ellen, featured in numerous issues. Every story painted the Hunters as among Highland Park's most charitable residents. Pillars of the community. Martin was a generous businessman and philanthropist who sought to do good with his hundreds of millions.

Looking at the time, I realized if I didn't leave then, I'd miss seeing Jessica, my wife, before she left for the hospital. We worked opposite shifts then, and were lucky to see each other a combined hour a day during the week.

"Hey, Oliver. We're headed out for drinks. Wanna come?" Bruce asked.

"Sorry, can't tonight. Rain check?"

❖

Friday morning, I drove straight to Mr. Wong's house. The salon didn't open till 10, so I hoped to catch him before he left.

On the drive over, I thought about the twenty minutes Jessica and I shared last night before she went to work. I told her my concerns about the salon story. She listened, but didn't offer much besides sympathy. Fair. To her, understanding media ethics was like me grasping antibiotic regimens.

Mr. Wong's home was a small ranch, blocks from White Rock Lake and in an older section of town. The driveway was empty. I rang the doorbell. No answer. Knocked three times. Same.

I stepped off the concrete porch and searched for movement inside. No luck. I tried calling him again. Straight to voicemail.

"Hi, Mr. Wong. This is Oliver Scruggs. I'm a reporter for *Park Cities News*. I need to speak with you about a story I'm writing concerning an accusation a customer of yours has made against you. I really want to give you the opportunity to respond. I have to turn in the story today at 3 p.m. Please call me back when you receive this." I gave my number twice.

I left for the newsroom. Part of me wondered if Arch had given me such a tight deadline knowing it would be difficult to get comment from Mr. Wong in only a day and a half.

At my desk, I had emails waiting. The cosmetology board confirmed Mr. Wong had no prior disciplinary record. And corporate Fashion Styles provided a stern statement in essence saying they condemn all inappropriate actions by any employee toward their guests and would take swift action if an employee is shown in violation of its workplace code of conduct. I put it all in my story. Also added a placeholder saying Mr. Wong did not return messages seeking comment before press time.

The next few hours went by surprisingly fast. I ate a homemade sandwich at my desk for lunch. Tinkered with the story. Left more messages for Mr. Wong, both on his voicemail and at the salon, which said again they hadn't seen him today. I had the story wrapped by 1 with the exact headline Arch had strongly suggested. Not getting police comment irked me. I went to call several times but always stopped, Arch's rebuke echoing in my ear.

I killed time by researching Arch. Found out his father was an oil baron and the family was loaded. Old money. Arch went to Highland Park High and earned a master's in business at SMU. A Park Cities lifer. He bought *Metroplex Magazine* twenty years earlier, in '87, molding it into a premier publication covering entertainment, politics, and commentary on Dallas life.

"2:30 check," hollered Julie over the cubicles. "Everyone get your stories filed in t-minus thirty minutes."

Make or break time, Mr. Wong. As the story read, a highly regarded Highland Park resident accused Mr. Wong of groping her, and he declined to respond. Didn't look good for him. I wasn't torn because I thought he didn't do it. He probably did. I was torn because this felt rushed and calculated in some way by Arch and Carol.

3 p.m. came quick. I filed the story, still no word from Mr. Wong. I left to get some coffee in the breakroom. Bruce was filling a cup when I entered.

"Why so glum," he asked. "You filed your story, right?"

"Yeah. The salon manager didn't call me back. It's pretty one-sided."

"Did you quote multiple sources?"

"Yeah. Even got comment from the corporate office."

"Well, you did your job then. Know how many stories I've filed where the accused didn't comment? It's par for the course."

That made me feel a little better. We drank our coffees and Bruce shared stories of his time in journalism. Dude had written about so many cool events, including covering the night Kurt Cobain got punched in the face by the bouncer at Trees, a famous club in Deep Ellum.

"Drinks after the paper's put to bed?" he asked.

"Definitely."

When I got back to my desk, the red light on my phone was lit. I practically dove for it. But it wasn't Mr. Wong. It was Arch, asking to me to return his call.

"Oliver. Thank you for calling back. I reviewed the layout and wanted to congratulate you on a terrific story. No changes. Job well done, son."

"Thank you, sir."

I won't lie, the praise felt good.

❖

Jessica and I had a great weekend exploring Dallas. While I'd grown up in the Metroplex, she only went to nursing school there. On Saturday, we toured the Sixth Floor Museum, and had lunch at the Highland Park Soda Fountain, an old-timey diner known for its burgers and milkshakes. They were celebrating 95 years, so I got a jump on getting quotes with the plan of pitching a feature.

Walking into the newsroom on Monday, I felt good. The soda fountain story would be fluff, but the place was an institution and we had to do a piece on it. When I reached my desk, however, a padded manila envelope awaited me, the contents offering a career-maker story.

A stack of hastily taken photos. Most were fuzzy, but the clear ones showed an expansive home library filled to the rafters with Nazi artifacts and memorabilia. Two Nazi flags hung on either side of a massive display in the center of the room. The sight of the swastikas made me sick to my stomach. I flipped through the stack, found close-ups of items. A landscape painting with a brass tag on the frame indicating Hitler as the artist. Nazi propaganda pamphlets. A signed copy of *Mein Kampf*. On and on. The last three photos identified the owner of the library. Bill envelopes with Martin Hunter's name. An exterior shot of the mansion with the address shown. And a photo of a wall-sized portrait of the Hunter family.

Bingo.

I pumped my fist. Searching the manila envelope, I found a note with the construction worker's name and phone number. Proof and a source. I stuffed the photos back in the envelope.

Our pitch meeting wasn't for another ten minutes, but I was so excited I sat in the conference room alone, taking notes on who to interview, what avenues to explore.

But when I actually pitched the story, Cliff swatted it out to half court. He didn't even look at the photos I spread on the table. A "non-starter," he said. Arch wouldn't allow it. I had no idea what he meant. I was furious, but not wanting to create a scene, I excused myself and went to my desk.

Later, after the meeting ended, Bruce stopped by my cubicle.

"Don't take it hard. Hunter's Nazi collection is an open secret. We've all pitched it one time or another and Arch always shoots it down."

"But why? I have proof!"

He shrugged. "Good ol' boy network. Who do you think Arch bought the magazine from? Those two were college roommates."

"Seriously?"

"Yep. Rich, old-money HP kids. Even if they weren't tight, it's not like Arch has objectivity on the matter."

"What do you mean?"

"I mean . . . have you seen his office? All the African stuff? And there's rumors he may have some goosestepper shit back at his place, too."

"You're fucking kidding me," I said.

"Don't run with it, but yeah."

Right then my phone rang.

"Excuse me, Bruce." He shuffled away. "This is Oliver."

"Oliver. It's Arch. Cliff tells me you pitched a not-so-sensitive story this morning."

"Yeah, he said you wouldn't allow it."

A long pause. "It's not the right time."

"What's that mean?"

"I need you to interoffice those photos to me."

"Seriously?"

"Thanks for your hard work, Oliver." The phone went to dial tone.

❖

I didn't send Arch the photos. Instead, I stewed the rest of the day. How the hell could he deny us reporting that one of the city's most influential businessmen and philanthropists had a Hitler fascination? Not reporting it was a breach of everything I'd ever learned about journalism.

It was about an hour from quitting time when I received a call on my cell phone.

Kim Wong.

In broken English, a very panicked Mr. Wong told me how he'd been fired and his cosmetology license suspended, pending a state investigation. A solid follow-up story for me. Then, he told me something that shook me. That he and Carol Winston had been having a consensual affair. Arch had found out about the affair, and this was his way of getting back at Mr. Wong. Something in his voice made me believe him.

Before we hung up, I told him I couldn't promise anything. He said he just wanted me to know the truth. Good thing, because Arch would never allow me to print this version.

I was furious.

I felt manipulated, used.

Arch had clearly wielded the newspaper like a weapon to settle a personal vendetta. And my byline topped the corrupted piece.

I snatched up the manila envelope of Nazi photos and stormed to the elevator.

The fifth floor was dark, and I feared I'd missed him.

But his desk lamp was on. The back of his chair faced the door. I tucked the envelope in my waistband behind my back and knocked hard on the glass. Then entered.

The chair swung around. "Oliver. You startled me. What can I do for you?"

"How can you cover up Hunter's Nazi artifacts?"

"Cover up? Son, not reporting something isn't the same as covering it up."

"That's exactly what it means."

He rocked in his chair. His expensive cologne wafting off of him. The contents of the room suddenly felt like they were closing in on me. Creeped me out. Not because of the art itself, but because this old, rich white guy surrounded himself with artifacts from a culture that was distinctly opposite his. And he protected a friend with artifacts that likely bolstered both of their disgusting belief systems.

"Where are the photos, Oliver?"

I scoffed. "What happened to uncovering ugliness?"

He just smiled.

"You should also know I just got off the phone with Kim Wong and he told a very different story about what happened with him and your wife. He says you found out they were having an affair. Is that true?"

"Boy, how dare you come in here throwing attitude at me. Do you know who I am?"

"I know you're compromised."

He laughed at that. "You know what? We don't require your services any longer."

"You're firing me?!"

"Things just didn't work out like we'd hoped."

"You can't do that!"

"Of course I can. Texas is an at-will state." Glee danced in Arch's eyes. "Besides, you were on a 90-day trial. Pack up your things and security will escort you out of the building."

My jaw would have hit the floor in shock if my lips weren't so tightly pursed.

"Fuck this." I stormed out.

True to Arch's word, a security guard was waiting for me at my desk. I didn't have much to gather, just my lunch bag, messenger bag, and some notebooks.

Once outside, I stood in disbelief.

My phone rang. Caller ID said it was the newspaper. I answered.

"Mr. Scruggs, this is human resources. Mr. Winston would like to offer you a year of pay in exchange for your discretion."

"Meaning what?"

"If you come back in and sign a non-disclosure agreement and hand over the materials in your possession, we can process a one-time payment of $25,000."

On one hand, a year of salary would be hard to turn down. On the other, I'd corrupted myself enough for one day. "Tell Arch to get bent."

❖

I didn't waste any time when I got home in reaching out to the Park Cities beat reporter at *The Dallas Morning News*. I filled her in about Martin Hunter, and how Arch had covered for him and may himself be in possession of Nazi artifacts. She pounced on it, as I expected. We met up an hour later at a coffee shop and I lent her the photos. She was appalled. Said she'd chase down the rest, and thought her editor would greenlight the story for Sunday's front page.

The rest of the week dragged.

I occupied my time by contacting other newspapers about openings. Nothing doing in Dallas County. I did land an interview with a weekly newspaper in Carrollton, although I'd take a $5,000 hit on the starting annual pay if I got the job. Adding insult to injury, I received my one and only check from *Park Cities News* in the mail on Friday. Less than $500.

When Sunday finally arrived, I ran to the newspaper machine at our apartment office and clunked in five quarters to get a copy of the Sunday edition.

I hurriedly unfolded it. Nothing above the fold. But there at the bottom of the front page was the story. The piece that would take down Hunter and Arch by exposing the wickedness running through the upper echelon of Park Cities society.

Only, the headline read: "Former SMU roommates Hunter and Winston elevate profile of Dallas philanthropy to great heights."

I plopped down on the curb.

All I could see was red and Arch Winston's sick smile staring back at me.

"Real money was just for show apparently. But what difference did that that make to the gunman anyway? He had something to walk out with."

$600 Ski Mask

Tim P. Walker

I t was the eyebrows. That was the first thing Ajay noticed. Narrow and arching, full and brown as the man's beady eyes, not a hair askew or out of place—the kind of eyebrows that never caught a speck of gutter dust on a windy day. Ajay could picture a tiny comb dragged across them each morning. Ten strokes per brow. Twenty perhaps. Granted, groomed eyebrows weren't a rare sight in that part of Pershing Park, even at the Lucky Stop convenience store on Cavanaugh Mill Road. It's just that these eyebrows happened to be sticking out from the eyehole of a sleek black knit ski mask that covered the man's head.

Ajay thought he must've hit the vape pen a little too hard. Dressed head to toe in pressed black clothing, including the mask, nothing about the man before him seemed real. But then he remembered that this was the night. And this had to be the guy.

As the hollow electric chime of the entrance alert faded and the front door swung shut, the masked man glanced quickly over his shoulder at the empty parking lot outside. Before Ajay could ask him if he needed help, a manic spark flashed in the man's eyes as a gun appeared in his leather-gloved hand. A pair of high sharp cheekbones pierced the eyehole of his mask like a pair of flicked switchblades. The moment the man leveled the gun on him, a ripple of fear rushed through Ajay and he found himself reaching into the pocket of his green smock for the remote panic button, the one that would signal the alarm company, who would then summon the police. If the gun was a fake, it didn't look it. It didn't matter if the man hadn't meant any real harm either—that gun was pointed at *him*. As the man marched to the checkout counter, Ajay raised his hands and backed away from the cash register.

"Okay, bitch, you know what's up," the man said in an airy tenor, each word forced through the fabric of his mask threatening to collapse under the weightlessness of his voice. Like Ajay, he was a lean man, and the height strip that lined the metal frame of the front door had clocked him at a few ticks over five feet. The gun, a boxy-looking thing of average size, dwarfed the arm that held it, and it trembled as the man tapped the side of the cash register with the barrel. "Let's go, Habib. Empty that thing."

Hah-beeb? Good god.

Whatever tingle of dread Ajay felt completely fizzled. Of course this was the guy. And he had to be one of those types, didn't he? It didn't matter if the name tag pinned to his smock spelled it out with two simple letters—*A-period J-period*—this asshole was going to call him whatever he felt like calling him. With jerks like these, it was either Mohammad or Osama or Mustafa. Closest they came was when they called him Apu, which at least was an Indian name.

The man leaned over the counter and shook the gun in Ajay's face. "Hurry, bitch!"

Ajay nodded and bit back any urge to scowl or scoff. He lowered his hands and tapped the button on the register that read *No Sale*. When the drawer shot out and all the coins in their trays rattled like death's chains, the man nearly jumped out of his skin.

"Watch it, Habib!" He jiggled the gun. "This is loaded. If I want to, I could blow your caca brains out and nobody would do a damn thing about it."

Caca?

Despite his best efforts not to, Ajay must've squinted or made some kind of face because the man squinted back at him harder, as if to drill the meaning of the word *caca* into his brain, whatever that was. "Nobody would care," the man said.

Ajay shrugged and gestured at the register. "Sorry," he muttered. "It's this machine. It's old as shit." Older than himself he was sure, if not the gunman. Ajay's father wasn't one to replace things that weren't completely broke, and he'd owned the store since the nineties.

"Shut up. You're not supposed to talk," the man said. "Just hand that cash over already."

Ajay gingerly flipped the clips in the bill trays. Beginning with an inch stack of ones, he started laying out the cash on the countertop.

"What, are you new here? Put it in a bag!"

Ajay nodded and peeled off a bag that hung from a hook on the counter. Printed across the front in bold red letters were the words *THANKYOU*. As he started to stuff the ones in the bag, the man pounced again.

"Seriously? Plastic? What about paper?"

"Dude... sir, this all we have."

Sneering, the man sighed and waved the gun at the register. "Fine. Put it all in a plastic bag then. And stop talking."

Ajay slipped the rest of the bills from the drawer—a few twenties and a few fives—into the bag and started sifting through the coin tray.

The man slapped the counter. "Uh-uh, not those."

Ajay raised his hands and stepped back from the register. The man kept his eyes and the gun fixed on the clerk as he grabbed the bag from the counter. For a moment, it looked like he might turn and run. Maybe he'd throw in a command for Ajay to lay down and count to a hundred or whatever spiel he practiced.

Instead he stood there shaking the bag, which may as well have been stuffed with cobwebs. "You're joking. This can't be it."

Ajay had been told to horde as much cash as he could in the register that night, but how? He could've counted the number of cash-paying customers that he'd had all week on one hand, to say nothing of that night. It was like that any given night. At the end of most shifts, he'd close out the register with a thick stack of credit card receipts and not much more cash than what he'd just stuffed into the bag. Real money was just for show apparently. But what difference did that make to the gunman anyway? He had *something* to walk out with.

"What about the safe? You have one of those, right?"

Ajay let out an exalted breath and gestured to a spot under the counter beneath the case of lottery scratch-offs. But how was he supposed to tell him that he couldn't access everything in the safe because he didn't have the combination? The best he could do was press a button at the top which would spit out a couple of twenties in a plastic tube. That function was on a timer, so if the man wanted another couple of twenties, he would've had to wait another five minutes before Ajay could push the button again.

But the inner workings of the safe didn't concern the man at the moment. "Where are you pointing? At that thing?" With the gun, he pointed to the thing in question—the roller grill next to the scratch-off case, which at the moment had a trio of quarter-pound hot dogs spinning between the rows of Teflon-coated rods. By dawn, somebody would've bought one. Someone usually did. "The safe is under *that* thing? You can't be . . ."

His eyes narrowed and the mask crimped as his lip curled beneath it. "You're telling me that whoever manages this place would willingly store money in a spot where that garbage can ooze all over it."

Out of the corner of his eye, Ajay thought he spotted something dip below the front window just beyond where the magazine rack sat. Nothing, he thought. If there was a person out there, then they likely arrived at the same time as the gunman. Ajay was told they'd be around, but he wasn't supposed to see any of them. Phantoms at work. A real customer would've parked out front. Any cop would've parked out front, too. But the shimmer of the night's heat in the building's floodlights illuminated the dark emptiness of the parking lot.

The man held the bag by the tips of his gloved fingers. "Were any of these bills in that safe? Did that shit get on them?"

Ajay was drawn to the front windows again, but instead of a parking lot full of dark empty space, there was a face on the other side of the door crouched next to the sticker that read *We Card* with a pair of eyes intensely focused on the gunman. When the face saw that Ajay had spotted him, he raised a finger and pressed it to his lip.

Was he part of it? He had to be. The Lucky Stop graveyard shift brought the same array of characters nightly—from the big bearded guy who bought a pack of Parliaments and three bottles of Mountain Dew every night to the guy who asked for a razor whenever he purchased a pack of Swisher Sweets. But those folks and just about every other customer who walked through that door were white, and the reality of Pershing Park was that you could count the number of black faces you'd see in that neighborhood on one hand. The face at the door, a man with dark skin and peppery short-cut hair—he wasn't one of those numbers.

So if he was part of it, Ajay thought, what was his role? Was he a hurdle? A challenge? Part of the experience? From what little Ajay knew of the gunman, he figured a guy grossed out by hot dog juice probably had less of a stomach for surprises. Still, as he opened his mouth, a thought tickled his brain—how profoundly stupid it would be to say anything at all at that point.

Damn how he'd wish he didn't open his mouth.

"Heads up, man," Ajay said and he nodded at the front door. The electronic bell rang out overhead as the door opened and the face tore across the store like a bull loosed from its pen. The gunman turned his head in time to catch the face barreling at him, and a high-pitched shriek pierced the mask as the guy connected, plowing right into the gunman's side. The impact sent them both crashing into a rack of potato chips that lined the front counter, and the force of their bodies made one of the bags explode with a loud violent burst.

Except, no—it wasn't a bag, because potato chip bags don't pop that loudly, do they?

The gunman jumped up screaming with something dark and wet running down the front of his pressed black trousers. He pointed his gun at the floor and fired it. Once, twice, three times—the muzzle flashing a blinding white light with each shot as deafening cracks erupted and the store filled with smoke.

That gun—it was real?

And loaded? Actually loaded? And when he pointed it at Ajay, it really was . . .

"Fuck!" the man screamed as he ripped his mask off and fired two more rounds at the floor. His whole body recoiled with each shot until he'd shoved himself against the end of one of the shelves behind him. His face had a tint of bronze that likely could've been slapped on there at the tanning salon next door, and his hair was a slick mat of lacquered blonde strands that looked like it hadn't been bottled up in a ski mask at all.

"Who is he? Who sent him?" he said. His beady eyes looked more frenzied with his gaunt face unbound.

Ajay could feel his nerves melt as he stood stiff, numb. His eyes darted between the gunman and some space out of sight on the other side of the counter. Mister Sneaker-Upper. He was there. On the floor.

And he was fine, too. Ajay was sure of it. Any second the guy was going to jump to his feet with his fingers pointed at Ajay. The gunman was going to point his, too. Then one by one, everybody involved with this charade were going to file in with their fingers all pointed at Ajay and everybody was going to laugh and cheer because the whole thing was one big prank and they got him. Got him good.

But the only thing pointed at Ajay was that man's gun, and he wasn't laughing. "I said, who is he?"

Ajay shook his head and jammed his hands into the pockets of his smock. One hand wrapped around the panic button. Some voice in the corner of his brain screamed for him to push it; that he was out of his depth, the button was his only life preserver, and if he didn't press it now he'd be sunk. His other hand wrapped around his vape pen, fully-loaded with liquid salvation, the thing that kept him floating most nights from ten until dawn. He couldn't find the strength in his arms to draw either thing.

The gun trembled as the man winced and caressed his elbow. "Who?" he said, his voice cracking.

Hands raised, Ajay backed up until he was pressed against the rack of cigarettes. "I don't know," he felt himself try to say, but he couldn't draw the breath to speak. His head grew heavier, his knees shakier, and the more he thought about what lay on the other side of that counter, the more the floor's cold blue tiles seemed to swell between his toes.

The chime rang out again, and a scruffy man with greasy, curly hair dressed in a plain black t-shirt and baggy charcoal jeans nearly stumbled over himself coming through the door. He stuffed his fist in his mouth when he saw what lay in front of him.

Another man barged in behind him and pushed him aside as he rushed to the counter. He too was dressed in dark clothing, only his pants, like the gunman's, were pressed black slacks. Over his black t-shirt he wore a grey fleece vest. His face was clean shaven. On his head was a fitted baseball cap and a pair of thick-rimmed glasses. Unlike these other men, Ajay had met this man there at the store a few days earlier. His name was Robert and he told Ajay that if all went well, he wouldn't see him again. Then he slipped Ajay an envelope full of cash.

"Jesus," he said. He turned to Ajay. "What happened? You were supposed to keep the store clear."

Ajay felt the floor swelling to his ankles. *Keep the store clear?* No, this guy—Robert—specifically told him to *do nothing*. Don't talk, don't eat, don't drink, don't smoke, definitely don't call the cops, and, above all, don't plan. See, the client—the man with the mask and the gun—he was going to need that element of surprise, that spontaneity, everything that made it feel real. So no, Ajay wasn't supposed to do anything to make it look like he was ready for this guy to show up and shove a gun in his face.

"It's not my fault," the client said, no mask to filter his nasally whine. "This is not . . . Look, this fucking ape just came at me from out of nowhere. I had to do it."

"Do what?" Robert said. "*You* shot him? With that?" He pointed at the gun, which hung limply from the client's hand. "That thing's loaded? With real bullets? Jesus, you weren't supposed to . . . Fuck." He grabbed the sides of his ball cap with both hands and pulled it tight over his temples. "Oh, we're so fucked right now," he moaned. "We are not insured for this. At all."

"I told you, it's not my fault," the client said, his voice so weightless that it could've floated away if a strong breeze blew through. "He came out of nowhere, and this one . . ." He shook the gun at Ajay as some heft crept into his throat. "This one warned me. This one told me he was coming. *Heads up*, he said. Right? So if anything, it's as much his fault . . ." He sneered and clamped his jaw shut, as if trying to swallow something that wasn't to his taste. "No," he spat. "Actually, it's his fault completely."

"You warned him?" Robert said to Ajay with his arms crossed. "So he *was* hiding out in here? That's what you're telling me, A.J.?" The way his tongue attacked those syllables, Robert could've been any customer reading the name on his tag in a pointed manner—one who thought that the coffee wasn't hot enough or the ice from the soda machine wasn't cold enough or the newspapers weren't new enough.

Or one who thought the robbery haul was too light and the man on the floor was too . . .

Dead?

Was he dead? God, he couldn't be, could he?

"No, man," Ajay said and he pointed his finger at the door and the darkness beyond it. "He was standing right there."

"Bullshit," Robert said. "We had eyes on the lot. You're gonna stand there and tell us he just strolled in here undetected?"

He turned to the scruffy guy, who was still eating his own fist. "Burke, you see anything?"

Burke shrugged. "Shit, I don't know. Ask Chand."

"Where is she anyway?" Robert marched to the door, and the chime rang its hollow note as he stuck his head out and called for the other crewmember.

Ajay watched her slowly shuffle into view outside from around the side of the building. She was dressed like the others, but her black t-shirt was tight, as were the pair of jeans that were ripped at the knees. She had a round face, brown skin, and her long dark hair was braided into pigtails. That her eyes were glowing red told Ajay that she'd either been crying or, like he so often was, surviving the night shift the best way she knew how—with a fully-loaded vape pen.

She took a quick peek through the window, then she immediately shook her head, turned around, and scuttled back out of sight.

"Chand, get in here," Robert called out gruffly. "We don't have time to fuck around, so you're either in here now or you're finished."

Her soft voice drifted through the open door, too faint for Ajay to make out what she said.

"*Finished* as in never-gonna-work-in-the-entertainment-biz-again finished," Robert shouted.

She dawdled back out from her hiding spot, but Robert wasn't waiting for her. He let the door shut as he turned and stepped back toward the counter. Eyes closed, he rubbed circles in his temples and spoke. "I need a couple of those bags you got back there, A.J."

He turned to Burke again. "Listen, I . . ."

He fell silent as a pair of headlights cut a swath through the darkness along on Cavanaugh Mill Road and crisscrossed the streetlight beams by the lot entrance. Both men stood frozen as their eyes followed the car until its red taillights faded.

"I need you out in the lot," Robert continued with a breathy sigh of slight relief. "If he isn't lying, then that means either you or Chand fucked this up and right now I trust your eyes more than I trust hers. Any civilians pull up—steer them the fuck off. Tell them that there's some kind of situation going on in here and they're closed for the rest of the night. If any cops show . . ."

As Robert muttered about how fucked they'd be anyway, the client paced the candy aisle, grinding the heels of his black Alexander McQueen tennis shoes into the tiles as he clutched his elbow and moaned curses to himself.

Stumbling out the door, his baggy charcoal jeans sagging below his waist, Burke nearly knocked Chand over. She herself shielded her eyes and sobbed under her breath as she entered.

As soon as she was in reach, Robert raised his arm and brought the back of his hand down on top of her head. It didn't make much of sound, but she whimpered softly and staggered away from him.

"Get it together!" he snarled. "You were supposed to be watching out for traffic. How'd this happen?"

"I don't know," Chand cried. "I didn't see him."

"Bullshit. He didn't just materialize out of thin air. Where'd he come from? Where's his car?"

"I don't . . . I didn't see any car pull up. He was just . . . there."

"Where?" Robert pressed.

With her eyes clamped shut, she pointed to the spot on the other side of the door. "He must've walked here," she sputtered.

"Walked? From fucking where?" Robert turned to Ajay. "I thought nobody walked around here. That's why we picked this . . ."

Ajay thought he felt the floor swelling up to his shins, so he threw up his hands and backed away before Robert could reach across the counter and smack him too. He needed to get out from behind it, if not the store itself, before the tiles cracked and swept him under completely. By the time he reached the corridor which led to the backdoor, Robert was reaming Chand out again.

"What do think you're doing?" the client yelled from between the soda fountain and the coffee counter. "You can't do that in here."

Ajay hadn't noticed that he'd taken the vape pen out of his pocket and snagged a puff.

"What's the problem, sir?" Robert asked.

"The problem is that this caca-brained idiot thinks it's okay to puff his peace pipe right now."

"Are you out of your mind?" Robert yelled at Ajay. "I need you focused. Do you realize how fucked you and your family are right now? You people could lose everything. *Everything*!"

"*Could*?" the client jumped in. "No—*will*." He stabbed the air with the barrel of his gun. "He will lose everything because I am suing him for everything."

"Whoa, sir, no," Robert said as he waved his arms and shuffled sideways past the front counter to step between them. "Look, it pains me to bring this up, but you did sign a contract, and that contract specifically stipulated that live ammunition not be used, okay?"

The client stirred and let out a growl that seemed to be aimed at Ajay.

"Now hold on, sir," Robert went on, his voice raised but calm. "Trust me here. I can fix this. Nobody has to sue anybody. Nobody has to get into any trouble whatsoever. If you could please, I need you to take your gloves off and rub your fingers across the barrel and grip of your weapon." He snapped his fingers and beckoned the girl standing by the front door. "And Chand is going to come over here and collect both the gun and your mask. Aren't you, Chand?"

They both did as they were directed. As the client peeled off his gloves and rubbed his fingers over his gun, Chand circled past the magazine rack, past the beverage coolers at the far side of the store, and around the coffee counter, circumventing the space in front of the checkout counter.

Ajay gripped his vape pen tight as he peered around the hot cheese urn atop the condiment bar next to the front counter, and gazed upon what lay on the floor. First he saw the peppery gray hairs and the wrinkly creases across the man's forehead. An older guy—did he not notice that before? How old could he have been? Old enough to have fought in a war? When he held his finger to his lip—was that a signal he would've given to his comrades in battle, leading an ambush on enemy soldiers—terrorists dressed in masks just like the one the client had on?

Ajay saw the man's dulled eyes, both of which were turned to Ajay. Those eyes, they seemed to be pleading, asking Ajay do to something. Anything.

Holy shit! Did he just blink? Ajay wondered if he'd hit the vape pen too hard again or if that man on the floor was actually . . .

Alive?

A chill ran down his spine as he heard a choked, soggy moan, but he couldn't tell if it came from the man on the floor or from his own head.

Chand must've heard it too, because a look of horror flashed on her face as she stared at the ground.

"Chand," Robert said, snapping his fingers, "take those bags I gave you and wrap your hands with them. Our friend here is going to hand you his gun and mask. Whatever you do, don't get your own fingerprints on them." He pointed at the man on the floor. "I want you to press as much of that gun as you can against his palms and fingers. Press it good. When you're done with that, take the mask and try to slip it over his head."

"Are you insane?" the client snapped. He clutched the mask to his chest as his grip on the gun tightened. "You can't give this to him."

"Sir," Robert said, "please . . ."

"No," the client pressed, and some heft crept back into his throat as he shook the mask crumpled in his hand. "This is a six-hundred-dollar balaclava. It's Prada. It's worth more than his entire fucking wardrobe. And you think you can just . . ."

"Okay, sir," Robert jumped in. He laid a gentle hand on the client's shoulder. "Of course. You're absolutely correct."

"Hey," Chand said, her voice creaky as she pointed down. "He's moving."

Ajay's gaze fell back on the man on the floor. He watched the man writhe and stretch his upturned hand toward Robert, as if to beg the director of this charade for another chance.

"Jesus!" Robert shouted, noticing the man's encroaching hand. He yanked his foot away.

The client wasn't as close, but he nonetheless scuttled backwards past the coffee station and further away from the man he shot.

"Moving? What do you mean *moving*?" He waved his hand, flinging his mask as if using it to swat mosquitos. "Make it stop doing that!"

"Chand, just take one of those bags and put that over his fucking head already," Robert said as he danced on one foot, inspecting the hem of his trouser leg in a spot where he thought the man might've touched. "Put him out of his misery. I mean, seriously, do I have to think of everything?"

Ajay locked eyes with the dying man again. Nothing in his vape pen could ever trick him into imagining a look so desperate, so pleading. He could almost feel the floor tiles buckle and swell and something cold coil around his knees. He pulled the panic button from the pocket of his smock and held it out like it wide like it might explode. "Stop," he called out. "You can't do that to him. You just can't. I gotta . . ."

"Whoa, *Aidge*," Robert said, merging the two syllables on Ajay's nametag as if they were business acquisitions that needed downsizing. "Chillax, buddy, we're taking care of it."

"Please stop," Ajay said, struggling to push the words out for lack of breath. "Just leave him alone. We gotta get, like, an ambulance for him. Something."

But Robert moved in on Ajay, and he calmly grabbed his wrist and nudged him backward into the darkened corridor. Still locked in on the Ajay, he called out over his shoulder to Chand and told her to proceed with all that he told her to do.

He dropped his voice to a whisper and, nodding slowly as he spoke, said, "Aidge, buddy, look, I'm sorry I've been cross with you. Obviously, this is a stressful situation, and we really need to pull together or else it will ruin all of us—you, me, Chand, Burke, our client, your family. I mean, how long have they owned this place? Thirty years? For you guys to lose it all now over this . . ."

Ajay felt his throat tighten. Somewhere behind Robert the client paced the aisles as Chand bent over the man on the floor, knees trembling as she dangled the pistol pinched in her plastic bag-wrapped fingers over the man's limp hand.

"Besides, who was that guy anyway?" Robert said. "I get that he thought he was helping. I do. But who was he really? Some guy who just happened to be walking by? In this neighborhood? Really? For all we know, he wanted to rob this place himself. Like, for real rob it. And now we're supposed to let him ruin *our* lives?"

Ajay stirred slightly, and Robert placed his hand dead in the center of his chest and shushed him before he could speak. "Look, Aidge, I'll tell you what," he said in a near whisper. "Are you familiar with that empty shopping plaza on Route 42 going west out of Cottswald City? Been empty for the better part of a year now. See, right in the middle of it is a bank building, used to be a First Traders. Still has a vault and those drive-through tubes and all the fixtures and everything. Anyway, as we speak, I'm lining up a stable of investors who are going to help me reopen the place. I'm talking tellers, managers, safe deposit boxes, lollipops for the kids, and a ton of cash on hand. The difference though—get this—it's not going to be a real bank. See, the only customers we're catering to are guys like our friend there." He threw a nod over his shoulder to the client, still pacing the aisles. "Buddy, you have no idea how many guys like him there are in the world—guys who'll pay obscene amounts of cash to shove a gun in a pretty girl's face and pretend to be a hard-ass for a little while without, you know, consequences or whatever. Now I haven't told anybody else here about this place, but I'm telling you this now because I want to offer you a spot on the ground floor of this venture. Now I know you don't want to work for your father all your life, right? If you did, you wouldn't have taken that offer when I made it, now would you? Wouldn't have taken the cash. Look, all I need from you right now is to cooperate and do everything I tell you. Okay?"

Ajay glanced past Robert, but he couldn't see the client or Chand or the man on the floor anymore. What he could see—all the many would-be heroes that were going to find themselves in the same position, sprawled out on a blue-tiled floor in a fake bank while a handful of girls with nametags on their cardigans shield their teary eyes as another Chand plants a gun and a knit mask—maybe something cheaper than the Prada balaclava that the gunman who shot him walked in wearing. Meanwhile, the bank manager, dressed in a crisp white shirt with a striped tie, would be nearby shaking the gunman's hand, calling him a hero.

Just like what Robert was doing with his client at that moment.

"Go ahead and summon the police now, Aidge," he said. "Remember—that guy was holding you at gunpoint when our friend here rushed in, tackled the assailant and wrested the gun from him, shooting him in the process. Got it?"

Ajay couldn't dig the panic button out of his pocket fast enough, but no matter how hard he pressed it, the floor wouldn't steady beneath his feet, and he felt the coldness creep up his body until it was around his chest. In a few minutes, a dozen flashing lights would be lined up outside his father's store, pouring in through the glass in a blinding torrent of reds and blues, the same glass the man on the floor had peered through a short time before. And the cops would soon be standing over that man's body, poking it, prodding it, and peppering Ajay with all kinds of questions about the man and what he must've done to get himself shot. Somehow Ajay knew that no matter what he told them—the truth or Robert's scripted lie—it wasn't going to matter. The client was going to tell his own story, and that story was the one that was going to stick. A man with groomed eyebrows, whose hair never mussed and pants never wrinkled, whose villain mask came with a designer label—could bad things ever cling to a man like that? Ajay couldn't even see the spot on the client's trousers where the dead man's blood spilled anymore. And he himself hadn't laid a single finger on the poor man, yet the sight of those pleading eyes and that limp outstretched hand flooded his thoughts as the iciness coiled around his throat.

Just to stay afloat, Ajay pulled out his vape pen and took another hit, but there wasn't much salvation left in there either.

12

"*Would you do anything, anything, for your mother?* I had asked them both and Simon had been the first to say, *Yes yes Mommy, I would do anything for you.*"

The American Way

Jesse Lee

I'm the perfect mother.

The reason both my sons are so successful is because all their lives I've worked to instill in them this simple, easy-to-remember, mandate: In order to rise to the top you have to cut out the competition. Cut out the threat. Cut out as in *eliminate*. This applies to both career and family. Make it your religion. If you stick to this approach, everything else will fall into place.

Not very nice, you might say, not enlightened, but it's the American Way. Winning at all costs. Think how obsessed Americans are with sports. In high school Simon played basketball and James soccer. I encouraged it because it helped get them into good universities and made them mentally tough. But after they got their college acceptances I made them quit. Because really, sports are just games. A waste of time. I won't even let them watch in the apartment when they come home.

As a first gen immigrant, you could say that I know the American Way from the outside in. My parents sent me to boarding school in the States when I was fourteen. I was devastated to have to leave my life in a major Asian city I will not name, the most civilized city in the world.

America had its own glamour of course, but those rich blond girls bullied me like you would not believe, day in and day out. Not in the obvious way boys do, but all that talking behind your back. Girls are sneaky. I am glad I never had a daughter.

Even if my last name wasn't a brand of jewelry, cosmetics, or cars, even if my family wasn't New York City Social Register or international royalty, my father could buy and sell most of these girls' families ten times over. At least he could back then. Our family was in shipping, and when I was in prep school it felt like my father owned the world. It wasn't until I was in college that we lost all our money.

I'm not a genius but since I wasn't interested in sports or drama or music, basically all I did at boarding school was study, enough so that I was in the top ten percent of my class and got into a small New England college no one would be ashamed to have on their CV. Because the school was co-ed I had a much better social life than in high school. Then, my junior year, that thing happened with my father. I would have had to go on scholarship but my mother's sister bailed me out. She was a pain in the ass, made me report to her every month and grudged me such a small allowance that I couldn't even eat out. Luckily by then I had a boyfriend who didn't mind paying for everything, including vacations.

Chris was a prince. Not literally, he was American. English and German ancestry, the type of Massachusetts blue blood who could trace his family back to a couple of Presidents. First son, Exeter, captain of the ice hockey team, from the same gene pool as those bitch girls who tortured me at prep school. But for all his smarts and privilege, Chris was amazingly simple. He had never dated a nonwhite person before. I was never the prettiest girl in the room, but to Chris I was Michelle Yeoh. I knew I had to hang onto him. He was my chance.

And believe me, I had pushback.

Especially from Chris's second cousin, whom I suspected had designs on Chris herself and made up rumors about my family being criminals. I took care of her. She had an eating disorder but could never resist luxury chocolates, especially a kind of heavy cream truffle that cost two hundred dollars a pop. *Oh just a little bite,* she would say.

A little bite, laced with the peanut dust I provided.

She didn't die, but she was never quite right in the head again. Anaphylactic shock leading to lack of oxygen to the brain. The lawsuit against the company dragged on for several years, but her parents finally scored a nice settlement.

Chris and I got married the summer he finished law school and zero people were happy for us—not my family, not his—though everyone put on a good show.

We held the ceremony and reception in neutral territory, an inn dating from the Revolutionary War in upstate New York. I had to buy my mother's airline ticket. My father was otherwise engaged and couldn't make it. Forget my younger siblings. They could just watch the videos.

By then I was making my way up the hierarchy in a major retail chain and earning more than you would think, not as much as if I were in finance of course, but I had some outside commissions, rich ladies who would pay me to personal shop. I might have inherited some of those clients from colleagues who did not do their due diligence or were obviously taking advantage of their connections. I made sure management heard about these infelicities and kept my own freelance career clean. That is, I used a separate identity for outside work.

I didn't hate my job, but I quit as soon as I got pregnant. Chris was on a partner track at a white shoe firm in the World Trade Center and some ancient grand uncle had bequeathed his Park Avenue apartment to us so we could afford my not bringing in an income. I had already decided I was never going to work again. My job in this life was to bring up my boys—James came right after Simon—and Chris would—between salary, bonuses, and family money—ensure everything else was taken care of. Because my sons were going to have the best.

Obviously you can't plan for every contingency. I did not know my father was going to lose all his money the year I turned twenty. I did not know that planes were going to crash into the Twin Towers and leave the boys without a father. Chris was there at 8 AM as always, to get a start on the day before the phones started ringing.

After, I have to say, that cold WASP family of his came through. Because I had the boys, and everyone loved the boys.

We stayed in that Park Avenue apartment and because I wanted them near, they went to D----- and not boarding school, as Chris and I had once discussed. I knew they would thrive in private school because they had that last name as well as brains and beauty and money. Biracial was starting to be a thing. It was cool. Maybe the other D----- parents did not like me, but I didn't care. My boys were popular so the parents put up with me. I didn't particularly want to hang out with those people anyway. I only attended the functions I absolutely had to, just long enough to show face, as the kids say.

One thing I knew for sure: my boys loved me. They would have done anything for me. They still would. Every night since their father died, they tell me so. When they were kids they would tell me before they went to bed, then by phone call, and these days by text. I am and always will be their main person. In fact after Chris died I dismissed the nanny because they were getting too attached to her.

Okay, so I don't have a ton of friends. I'm on Facebook and WeChat because my parents and my siblings and their families like to see how the boys are doing. My sons have never been to what they call the Old Country. They are much more familiar with Chris's family than mine, since we spend every Christmas and part of the summers on my in-law's private island off the coast of Maine. I don't go up every year, but Simon and James are fixtures.

I spend a lot of my time shopping. Not for things, as I once did for a living—I now have stylists and personal shoppers of my own—and how I look or how the apartment or our houses look isn't as important to me as it once was. I shop for real estate all over the world.

Not under my own name of course.

As Chris's widow I was okay financially but being nice to my old bitch aunt and thanking her every two seconds had turned out to be a good move. She was cheap in life and generous in death, made me her sole heir, something no one but my lawyers and accountants know. I have my own island now.

I have to admit that, maybe because I have no friends, or maybe because she's mellowed over the years and she spoils my boys, I've become quite fond of my mother-in-law. She will sometimes call to chat, always at a random time, like three in the morning. Since Chris's father died she's been living by herself in that huge house on the hill in a little town outside of Boston, basically a hermit. I think she's lost track of the real world.

But she was never a stupid woman, and still has periods of extreme sharpness. Like a couple of months ago when she said, in the middle of one of our late night calls, "Oh by the way, do you remember Poor Miranda?" No one ever just said "Miranda"—it was always "Poor Miranda." Of course I remembered Chris's anorectic cousin who almost died choking on a chocolate.

"Miranda? Is she still alive?" As if I didn't know she was in a long-term care facility in Hartford CT. As if I didn't know the names of her entire care team, her treatment plan, what medications she was on. A zombie in the peak of health. Ten million dollars well spent, or wasted, depending on your point of view.

"Oh yes. Apparently she's been much more coherent lately. The staff says she's been asking for family. Actually, dear, she's been asking for you."

This was not good news. Not many family members visited her anymore but when anyone would mention her I would casually ask how she was. Having actually been in the room when the incident occurred, I was the one who testified that she had forgotten to pack her EpiPen in her purse. Up until now when I asked, people would shake their heads. *The same. All she does is sleep or stare in front of her.*

"Are you sure she's asking for me?"

"Well she asked for Chris first. We had to remind her, you know. And since then she's been asking for you. Every day, they tell me."

"Wow. Okay. I can go up and visit then, it's been a while. It will be wonderful to see her, now that she's feeling better."

Of course I had never visited Miranda. The last time I had seen her was on a gurney being inserted into the ambulance.

It was time to call on the boys. One of the boys.

It was late spring. Simon was at Johns Hopkins for medical school. James was in his last year at Yale. Of my two sons, James had always been a little harder to handle. He had his own mind, like me. Simon was like Chris. And he was studying to be a surgeon.

I don't drive and I can't bear the train so I had our chauffeur take me to Baltimore. I would have preferred the Phantom but the Mercedes attracts less attention on the highway, not to mention on the streets of a not very safe city. Simon would not be thrilled to have his day suddenly interrupted, but what I had to say wouldn't take long. On the way down I did some research and figured out my game plan. Yes, I learned that expression from American sports.

When we were at the outskirts of the city I texted Simon but got no answer. I guessed he was in the library studying and had his phone turned off. Simon can do that, James can't. I had the chauffeur drop me off at my son's townhouse, told him to park the car in a garage and go see a movie. Simon's housemate, a cheerful woman from Ghana who is in the same program, answered the door. We had met numerous times before, in fact I had taken her to dinner along with other friends of Simon's. She said Simon was in a lab but would probably be back in an hour or so. I sat in the kitchen and drank coffee and shopped for luggage on my phone. I heard the housemate run down the stairs and she called out *Good-bye, good to see you* in her friendly way and then the door slammed. I took out my special phone and checked on some of my properties, first in the Caribbean, then Greece, then South America. On that same phone, which is not under my regular name, I started a To Do list.

"Mom what are you doing here? Is everything all right?" Simon dropped his knapsack on the floor when he saw me. I smiled at my handsome son, six three, not tall for an American basketball player but very tall for someone from my side of the family. His hair has a slight wave, like Chris's, and he has my husband's nose. His eyes are a mixture of us both, but his big mouth with the full lips is all mine. In the months after Chris died, James had acted out but Simon had clung to me. *Would you do anything, anything, for your mother?* I had asked them both and Simon had been the first to say, *Yes, yes Mommy, I would do anything for you.*

I said now, "Mommy needs your help" and his eyes that were a mixture of Chris and me filled with tears, just as they had on that September evening. I said, "This is the last thing Mommy will ever ask you to do. But no matter what happens, even if you never see her again, remember what she has told you about the American Way."

This is how I picture him most clearly now, my elder boy, the last time I saw him, in the darkening kitchen, tears on his face. Even more tears when I asked what I had to ask, but I could tell he didn't even think about saying no to his mother.

Such a clever boy.

But I am clever too, in my own way. I only told him what he needed to know in order for him to give me the instructions, to get me the vial and the syringe with the smallest gauge needle.

Neither Simon or James know Miranda existed. And the people at the long-term care facility do not know that I exist. Why would I have used my own name or looked like myself when I finally went to visit?

Poor Miranda got her ultimate beauty treatment. She will never be too fat or too wrinkled again. And of course I will see my sons in real life in a year or two, when this tiny fuss has died down. I only said *even if you never see her again* to Simon for dramatic effect. It's not like I'm hiding, just taking a break. They could find me if they really wanted. But it never hurts to be cautious. I'm relaxing in the tropics now but at a moment's notice I could relocate to the other side of the equator in a different time zone.

The preliminary cause of death was registered as heart failure. Cause of death undetermined. There's a chance Miranda's family could bring a lawsuit against the long-term care facility but so far I haven't heard anything. I don't think they will. I am sure they are secretly relieved she is permanently off their hands and just want to put the whole mess behind them.

I do miss my boys. I could have insisted Simon be the one to inject the concentrated Botox into the IV. But of course I would never. It wasn't his battle to fight. He'll do his own work later. Despite the tears, he knows how to survive. Both he and his brother have been well schooled. I made sure of that because I'm the perfect mother, and it's the American Way.

Matthew Somerville Morgan, "The American Juggernaut: Everything noble, patriotic, and progressive is crushed beneath the remorseless tread of that mammoth monster of corruption, cruelty, and fraud, the vampire rings of capital," 1873

"'Dr. Coleman, I have a lot of money . . . And what is
the point of having all this money if I can't use it to
give myself a better life.'"

The Last Kind Act

Sean Logan

Thom Burrows was all the way back in the butler's pantry when the doorbell rang. That was possibly the worst part of owning a large house. With his housekeeper Nadia out running errands ahead of the party, he would have to trek through the kitchen, the staff dining area, the formal dining hall and the foyer to find out who was bothering him.

It was certainly too large a house for one person. If he ever managed to settle down, get himself a wife and a few kids, he might appreciate that extra room, though he didn't see that happening anytime soon: he was still in his forties, plenty of time for that. So for now, all that space was little more than a nuisance.

He opened the front door to find a young man with short black hair, shaved on the sides, wearing a white dress shirt and black trousers. He was in his mid-twenties and fit, but with the dark eyes of someone older.

"Mr. Burrows?" the young man said. "Glad I caught you at home. I'm Arty, with White Linen Catering."

Thom pulled up his sleeve to check the time on his Rolex Daytona, then turned his eyes to Arty. "I wasn't expecting you for another couple hours."

"Yeah, I'm real sorry about that. Rest of the team's still coming at two. I just had a few things to drop off, if that's all right . . . If I'm not bugging you too much."

Thom sighed. "I suppose it's fine. There's a staff entrance around the side." He tipped his head toward the west wing of the house. "You can pull your van around."

Thom took the long walk back through the kitchen and opened the side door. Arty came in a moment later carrying two large sacks of ice. "Can you point me to the freezer?"

Sadly, Thom didn't have a standalone commercial freezer. It was an oversight. His brother Jack had a massive stainless-steel freezer, even though his house was a tenth the size of Thom's. But Jack was always hunting, so maybe he needed the space for all the woodland creatures he killed. Still, even though Thom wasn't invited to join him on those manly adventures, and wouldn't want to go if he were, there was no reason he shouldn't have a nice freezer too.

"I'm sorry, the Sub-Zero's entirely full," he said, seeing no reason he should admit his deficiency to this stranger. "Couldn't you keep that in your employer's freezer for now?"

"Yeah, no, I don't think we can," Arty said, shifting the cold bags in his arms. "Like I said, I'm real sorry. Our ice supplier is out here by you and I'm not heading back across town. Got a whole lot of errands to run out here while the rest of the crew gets all that good food prepped. Going to be quite a spread."

This was true. If there was one area Thom would spare no expense, it was the food. A party with great food and an open bar would always be considered a success. There could be a smallpox outbreak and a mass shooter, but if his guests had a foie gras canape in one hand and a stiff cocktail in the other, no one would complain.

"Do you have a bathtub maybe?" Arty said, fidgeting like he really wanted to set that ice down. "If we could stack the bags all together, they shouldn't melt too bad. And we won't need to worry about them dripping everywhere."

"Okay, fine, this way," Thom said, leading Arty through the kitchen toward the back of the house. "The guest suite here on the first floor has a bathtub. And speaking of dripping everywhere, try not to. A few drops on this marble floor, it'll be like trying to walk across an ice rink."

The guest suite was just off the library. He'd never actually used the suite before, but it had a nice, jetted tub big enough for two. Arty dropped in the sacks of ice then went back for another two, dripping water all through the kitchen, despite Thom's urging. After a third set of bags, when it really started bordering on overkill, he came in with something else, a small red and white Igloo cooler.

"I've got one more favor," Arty said, "but this one should be more fun." He set the cooler on the granite countertop of the kitchen's center island and removed two bottles of champagne. "Just a little taste test for the bar menu."

Thom finished his apple/beet/kale juice and put the glass in the washer—he'd have to remind Nadia to clean the Angel Juicer the second she got back, or it would be an impossible task. "Fine," he said, "but after this I need to start getting ready."

Arty grabbed two champagne flutes from Thom's glassware cabinet. "I'll be out of your hair in a hot minute."

Thom recognized one of the bottles as the Louis Roederer he'd previously settled on. The other appeared to be a French brand, the label written in an ornate script that was all but unreadable.

"Château Palissy," Arty said. "Normally goes for one fifty a bottle—if you can even find it. But our importer likes us. Let's just say a few extra fell off the truck. You like it, you can have it for four hundred a case. But first, just for comparison . . ."

Arty unclamped the stainless-steel stopper on the already opened bottle of the Roederer and poured a taste into one of the glasses. Thom tried it. He wasn't much of a champagne guy, but it seemed good. Certainly better than what most of his guests would be used to: with the possible exception of his Executive Leadership Team, he doubted any of the employees he'd invited had tasted anything that didn't come from the bottom few shelves of their local grocery store. And his brother? Thom had to make sure the bar was stocked with Bud Lite to accommodate Jack's refined sensibilities. Probably the only way he could get him to come, despite the occasion.

"And here's the Palissy." Arty removed the stopper from the other bottle and poured several ounces into the same glass.

This one Thom didn't care for. Maybe it was because it was French. It had an earthy, minerally quality—was that characteristic of a French champagne? Or maybe he just didn't have a sophisticated enough palate. Either way, he wouldn't be serving it, even if it was a relative bargain.

"I think we'll be sticking with the Roederer," he said, dumping the remainder of his glass into the sink.

"Fair enough. I'll go ahead and get out of your way then. Like I said, rest of the team will be by at two. I've seen what they're working on and it's going to be great. So, what's the big event, if you don't mind me asking? You celebrating something special?"

"My health," he said. "I had a kidney transplant a year ago today, and it went well, so I thought I'd invite some friends and family over to help me celebrate my good fortune."

Arty pushed the stopper closed on the Palissy. "Aw, that's just great. I'm glad to hear it. And I know you didn't ask or nothing, but I guess we both had some good fortune. This time last year things were pretty rough for me too. Living on the streets. I'll just say I had some trouble readjusting to civilian life after serving my country. Over in Iraq, I was a combat medic, helping save lives. Back home, I could barely take care of my own. Mental health, addiction issues. But now look at me—healthy, clean, employed. That sounds like some pretty good fortune to me. So, what do you say? A little toast?" He poured some of the Roederer into each of the two glasses.

Thom thought this was rather presumptuous for the help, but he didn't want to be a bad sport. He raised his glass.

"To our good fortune!" Arty said.

"Our good fortune."

They clinked glasses and drank.

"And that's great you got a kidney," Arty said. "I heard that's not so easy. I heard it takes a long time."

Thom knew that to be true. There were a lot of people who wanted—needed—a healthy kidney, and finding an exact match was difficult. It did take a long time. Usually. For most people.

❖

Dr. Coleman showed Thom back to his office. Thom had been seeing him for over fifteen years and didn't even know he had an office; they'd always met in one of the exam rooms. He didn't expect this to be good news.

He already knew he had kidney disease. They'd found too much albumin in his urine and creatinine in his blood. Now they'd taken a biopsy of the kidney to get a better idea of how bad it was.

Dr. Coleman took a seat behind his large, cluttered desk and Thom took the chair across from him. He didn't like that his doctor had a messy office. And his wispy silver hair always looked like he'd just come in out of the wind. He hadn't really thought about it over the years, but now that things were more serious, it did strike him as less than professional.

"We got the results of your biopsy back from the nephrologist," Coleman said, shoving aside a stack of unsigned prescriptions and setting the results down in front of him. "The outcome wasn't what we were hoping for. It's much farther along than I was anticipating. Your estimated glomerular filtration rate is below fifteen."

Coleman had already explained all of this, but Thom couldn't process it. "So what does that mean?"

"It means you've lost more than eighty-five percent of your kidney function. And it means we'll need to get you on dialysis. Your kidneys are not doing their job well enough to keep you alive. I'd also recommend getting you on the waiting list for a donor kidney. A transplant is a treatment, not a cure, and you'll still have to take care of yourself. But you'll have a better quality of life, fewer health risks, and you won't need to have your blood cleaned for four hours a day, three days a week for the rest of your life."

For Thom, this didn't sound like a terribly hard choice. "Yeah, let's get me on the waiting list. How long do you think it'll take?"

Coleman drummed a pen against the edge of his desktop as he considered. "Given your health profile and your blood type, I'd estimate it would be at least five years."

Thom nearly jumped out of his seat. Had he heard him right? "Five years? Do you mean months?"

Coleman shook his head. "No, I mean years. Unless you can get a living donation. We, all of us, only need one kidney to live. So if you know of someone, a friend or a family member who'd be willing to donate—"

Thom gave a grunt, like a laugh that had lost its will to live. "Jesus, doc, that's quite an ask."

"It's a hell of an ask. But it's also your best bet."

He thought about who he could possibly consider. Friends were a non-starter. He had the guys from the poker game, and his golf buddies, but he wouldn't ask them to borrow a five iron, much less a vital organ. No, the only real option was his brother Jack, and that wasn't much of an option. They'd been drifting apart ever since their dad died. And if he was being honest, it was mostly his own fault. The more his career took off, the less he called. Their lifestyles had just grown so different. Now they were down to spending Christmas and Thanksgiving together and that was about it. He didn't even get invited to Jack's kids' birthday parties anymore. How do you ask someone you only saw twice a year to literally give you a piece of themselves?

"I don't think it's likely," Thom said. "Is there another option? Can I buy a kidney? Like, if someone wants to make some money—a lot of money—by donating a kidney, could I buy one?"

Coleman drummed the pen on the edge of his desk. Tap, tap, tap. Tap, tap, tap. "No," he said. "It's illegal under the National Organ

Transplant Act. You can't encourage someone to donate their kidney by offering to pay for it."

So, that wasn't an option. But there was a pause. Coleman was thinking about something before he said no, and Thom thought he might be able to get it out of him. Coleman didn't seem to be overly cautious about following the rules. If Thom asked for enough oxycodone to choke a mule, Coleman gladly wrote him the script. If there was a back door here, he might be willing to open it.

"Dr. Coleman, I have a lot of money." He assumed he already knew this; it said right on his medical forms he was CEO of Lockhern Financial, the third largest employer in Marin County. "And what is the point of having all this money if I can't use it to give myself a better life. This money means nothing if I don't have my health. I want to spend it, and I assume there are a lot of people out there who would like to have it. Is there anything, any way at all, I can use my money to speed up the timeline?"

Coleman clicked his pen closed and set it on his desk. He leaned back in his chair and laced his fingers. "Yes, of course, there's always something that can be done. With enough money and a certain," he made a rotating gesture as he searched for the right phrase, "a certain moral flexibility, anything's possible. Money can't buy happiness, but it can buy just about anything else."

Thom locked eyes with him. "I'm not speaking theoretically here. I want to know if there's anything I can do, right now, to get a kidney."

Coleman reached over piles of journals and manila envelopes and loosely stacked papers to grab a business card from a small silver tray. "I'll tell you what—you go home and call everyone you can think of. Make that big, embarrassing ask. Hopefully someone will surprise you. But if they don't, after you've exhausted every possible option," he scribbled a number on the back of the card and handed it to Thom, "you can contact me on my personal cell."

Thom went straight home and poured himself an irresponsibly large glass of Macallan. He sat in front of the fire in his parlor and drank most of the glass while he gathered his nerve. He picked up the phone.

"Tommy?" Jack said. "What's going on, man? Wasn't expecting to hear from you. Everything all right?"

"Well," Thom started, then paused, not exactly sure how to begin. "Not really. You see, I've got . . . I'm going to need to get a kidney transplant."

"What? Really? I didn't even know you were sick. How long's this been going on?"

"A couple months. But it's gotten bad and . . . here's the thing. I need to get a kidney. I mean, I need to find someone to donate one. That's . . . that's why I'm calling."

There was a long pause on the other end of the line. Thom could hear Jack breathing slowly through his nose. "Are you asking me to give you one of my kidneys? Is that what you're asking me?"

Thom always felt small when he talked to Jack, the only person in his life who could make him feel that way. Thom would always be the little brother. He'd gone out and made a big life for himself, built a big career, bought the big house, but as soon as he got on the phone with Jack, he was right back to being the little brother again. And now Thom felt no bigger than a child. "Yes," he said. "That's what I'm asking you."

"How bad is this? I mean, are you going to die if you don't get one right away?"

"Well, I'm more likely to die. But no, I'm probably not going to die right away. I'll have to go on dialysis while I wait and see if they can find me a donor."

"So you can get a kidney? Like off some dead guy who's an organ donor?"

"Yeah, but it's really hard. It'll take years."

Jack sighed into the phone. "Look Tommy, I'd like to help you out here, but I've got to think about my family."

"I am your family."

"I mean my kids. What if, down the road, one of my kids needs a kidney and I don't have another one to give them."

"It's fine. I understand."

"Do you know what I mean? I just don't think—"

"I get it. It's okay."

"I'm sorry, man. Hey, that's Barb calling me for dinner. I've got to run. But hang in there, all right? We'll be pulling for you. And you can call me if you need anything. You don't need to be such a stranger all the time."

Thom hung up the phone and drained the last of his Scotch. He got Coleman's number out of his wallet and wrote him a text: "I'm out of options."

The next day, he was sitting across from Coleman at an out-of-the-way downtown Starbucks, trying to make casual conversation while he nervously spun the sleeve around his venti Americano, waiting for Coleman to bring up the real reason they were there.

"Okay, here's the deal," Coleman said at last, taking a pen and small sheet of paper from the breast pocket of his wrinkled dress shirt. He wrote down two numbers then pushed the paper across the table to Thom. "The top number is what it's going to cost you. That's not the cost of the surgery; that gets paid in the usual way, through your insurance and whatever you'd usually pay out of pocket. That number there is the cost to bump you up to the top of the list. The other number is where you wire that money."

Thom looked at the top number: $460,000. He may have stopped breathing for a moment. But he gathered himself. He could afford it. And he wasn't going to complain now.

"Two things about this," Coleman said. "One is you should start getting ready now. Make any necessary arrangements at work, in your personal life, whatever. I don't know exactly how long this will take, but after you transfer that money, it should be quick. When we get the organ, be ready to drop everything."

Coleman set down his coffee and gave Thom a sober look. "The other thing is, starting right now, I recommend you never bring up this transaction again. Don't spend another minute even thinking about it. And don't ever ask me any questions."

Thom couldn't help but think about it. He couldn't help but wonder if he was being conned. Even though he could afford it, it was still a hell of a lot of money. But he went forward with the plan. He moved some finances around, made an excuse to his financial manager and transferred the money. And less than two weeks later he got a call from Coleman. They had the donor organ. And the next day he was already in surgery. He hadn't been conned. It all worked out fine in the end.

◈

Thom and Arty finished their champagne toast.

"Okay then," Thom said, ready to start shoving the young man toward the door if he had to, "I really need to start getting ready for the party."

"Oh yeah, no problem," Arty said, clamping the stopper back on the Roederer. "I'll clean up and clear out, let you get to your business."

He put the two bottles back in the cooler, but when he exited through the kitchen's side door, he forgot to bring the cooler with him. Thom was about to chase after him to return it, but Arty burst back in carrying two more huge sacks of ice. If one thing was certain, it was that none of his guests tonight would have to suffer the indignity of a warm beverage.

"Sorry just got a couple more of these to unload."

"Fine, could you just see yourself out when you're done," Thom said and started heading for the stairs in the foyer. He called back, "And lock the door behind you please." He didn't love the idea of leaving this stranger alone in his house. But his house would be filled with strangers shortly when the rest of the caterers arrived, so there was no reason to worry over this one.

As he passed through the staff dining area, he heard a splashing sound from the back of the house, like one of the ice bags had spilled open. He turned on his heel and headed back for the guest suite to see what sort of mess the young man had made, and he nearly slipped on the wet floor from the boy's earlier carelessness. Thom was growing dangerously close to losing his patience.

As he entered the guest bathroom, there was another splashing sound and he saw that Arty was deliberately emptying a bag of ice into the tub.

"What do you think you're doing?" Thom said. "That ice will be contaminated. I can't serve that to my guests."

"Sorry," Arty said, dumping out the rest of the bag. "I just thought this way all that melted ice could drip straight on down the drain."

"Well, don't. Just leave it in the bag until we need it . . . Wait, what are you doing?"

Arty started to tear open another bag. "Right, sorry, I'll stop," he said, not stopping. "How are you feeling, by the way? You're looking a little tired."

"I'm fine. Now stop that and go. I'm asking you to leave."

Arty ripped open the top of the bag and started pouring it into the tub. "Are you sure? You're not looking so good."

Maybe it was the power of suggestion, but he was starting to feel a little woozy. "All right, if you don't leave, I'm calling the police."

Arty emptied the rest of the bag. "Maybe you should sit down before you fall."

"Okay, that's it." Thom turned to go grab his phone, but the room spun with him as he did. He started toward the kitchen but was unsteady on his feet and had to reach out and grab the wall for support.

"You know, a minute ago, we were talking about our good fortune," Arty called after him. "It was almost exactly a year ago someone took pity on me, a tall, bald man with long hands and thick glasses. He saw me sleeping on the street and offered to take me up to his room, give me something to eat."

Thom's head was starting to swim and his legs were feeling numb and rubbery. He stumbled toward the kitchen.

"It was just a small motel room, but I was real grateful. It was a cold night out there and I felt the chill down to my bones. He heated up a bowl of soup for me in the microwave, gave me a glass of bourbon to warm my blood."

Thom could see his phone on the kitchen's center island, next to the red and white cooler. He staggered toward it as Arty followed up the hallway behind him.

"And there must have been something in that whiskey because I went out cold. Didn't wake up until the next day. When I did, there was an envelope on the chair next to me, had ten one-hundred-dollar bills in it. That tall man left me a thousand bucks. And he'd taken my kidney."

Thom shuffled across the kitchen to the center island. He reached out for his phone. But the floor was still wet from the melting ice that had been trafficked through there. He slipped and fell flat to his chest, the side of his face bouncing off the marble.

"When I saw the bloody wound, I called an ambulance. I survived, obviously. And while I was in that hospital bed recovering, a friend came to see me, one of the men from my unit. And when I got out, he took me in."

Thom tried to push himself up, but he felt all of the strength drain out of him and he slipped back to his chest.

"Even though my friend was struggling himself, no insurance, barely a penny to his name, he took care of me. Bought my prescriptions, food. Got me back on my feet. It wasn't until later I found out what he was doing in my wing of the hospital that first day he came to see me. Kidney disease. How's that for a sick joke? I would have given him one of mine in a heartbeat, but now I didn't have an extra to give."

Thom felt Arty's hands around his ankles. He was being pulled back, sliding across the slick floor.

"And that's probably the only reason I spent the last year tracking you down. If it was just me, I probably wouldn't have bothered. All those hours looking for that tall, bald man. Once I found him, and your doctor, getting them to talk, that was easy. But the search leading up, month after month with almost nothing to go on, talking to every homeless person in every piss-stained alley and tent city in three counties. It's more than I would have done for myself. But it wasn't just for me. You took what should have gone to my friend, to my brother."

They reached the carpet of the guest room. Arty grabbed Thom under the shoulders and dragged him the rest of the way into the bathroom. He left and came back with the cooler. He took out the bottles and set them next to the tub, then he scooped in some of the ice.

"For transporting the organ."

Thom felt a screaming panic deep down inside himself, but it was buried under a rising sea of blurry confusion. "But," he mumbled, his lips nearly too numb to talk, "I didn't . . . I didn't do this to you. It was that . . . tall man. And my doctor who . . . hired him."

"No," Arty said as he started to unbutton Thom's shirt. "That tall man? If I'd been shot, you might say he was the bullet. And your doctor, he's like the gun. But you—you and your money—that's what pulled the trigger." He removed one of Thom's cufflinks then the other. "And besides, they don't have my kidney."

Arty slid Thom out of his shirt. "But don't worry. Before that tall man left with my kidney, he did one real nice thing for me. He put me in a tub of ice, and that helped keep me alive until the ambulance came. And I'll do the same for you."

As he sank out of consciousness and everything went black, Thom tried to find some comfort in that: in the final act of kindness. It was more than the young man had to do. And it was more than he deserved.

14

"If they thought you had money, they would let you get away with anything."

La Isle Flotant

Tom Andes

Sometimes—just for shits and giggles—he pissed in their fish. It was a joke, and you knew how nobody could take a joke these days. Besides which, they never knew, so what was the harm?

But the chef, Rodrigue, who they'd imported from a Michelin-starred dump in Normandy, he did not see the humor.

"This is 400 euros a kilo," Rodrigue said. "This is sushi grade fugu. You do not make pee-pee in sushi grade fugu."

"Ah, come on." Godfrey slapped his back. "Lighten up, will ya, Francis? These yobs aren't going to know the difference."

He had a table of MIT professors, former United States Presidents, and members of the British Royal Family waiting. He'd just learned that word—*yob*—from a British Prince, and he was trying it on for size.

Yeah, it was funny how you could serve these people shit on a stick—he'd done that, too—and if you told them that it was rare, expensive, or better yet, endangered, they'd gobble it down like it was manna from heaven.

"I know the difference," Rodrigue said in heavily accented English, "and that is enough."

"Well, fugu you," Godfrey said, Rodrigue's face souring as Godfrey undid his belt. "One call, buddy, that's all it would take. I'm sure Interpol would be very interested in knowing your whereabouts, even if we are, at the moment, in international waters."

They were, in fact, on what he liked to call his Floating Island—La Isle Flotant, like the dessert—anchored off the coast of the U.S. Virgin Islands, but that was one thing about money: it made you international, and wherever he went, he was untouchable.

Back in Normandy, they'd helped Rodrigue pay off a judge, so he could walk on child molestation charges. Even in France, 13 would get you 30. It was good to have something to hold over the guy's head when he didn't feel like making French fries.

"You would not do that, Monsieur," Rodrigue said, but Godfrey could see in the man's face he knew Godfrey would.

"Au contraire," Godfrey said, "mon sewer."

And he giggled. French was just so damn funny, like the name of that fish, fugu. Literally, mind-blowingly hilarious.

He was directing his stream into the fugu when his darling Mathilde came in.

"My dear Godfrey," the woman said, "whatever are you doing?" She came closer, peering over his shoulder, a glint in her eye. "Are you fucking the fish?"

He'd dropped trou, his pants around his thighs, shirttails covering his bare ass. He'd always had a sense of the theatrical. Came from his early years teaching high school English to the children of wealthy Manhattanites.

She sounded like she might've joined in if he were fucking the fish.

"Pissing in the fugu," Rodrigue exclaimed. "He is pissing in the fugu."

Except he said it with a French accent: *piss* coming out *peace*, all those *th* sounds coming out *z*, so it was funny.

Maybe fucking the fish wasn't a bad idea. He'd done things with Mathilde that would make a rock star blush, including something with a tiger shark that the members of Led Zeppelin had once done with a groupie. The woman had the most remarkable appetite, and she could give him a run for his money when it came to her depravities, all thanks to her rich, perverted dad for messing her up for life.

"It's a joke." Godfrey zipped up. "Just a little harmless fun. I had no idea the French were so hung up."

Mathilde rolled her eyes. "You know the French, dear: they love talking about sex more than they like doing it. Do you mind?"

She took the tray of fish then, lifted her red sequined dress, and copped a squat, Rodrigue covering his eyes, like the guy might faint at the sight of a grown woman relieving herself. What a boob, an absolute ninny!

Beneath them, the Floating Island rolled across a swell, and Godfrey's stomach lurched. Sounds carried up to them, the screams belowdecks. Were they louder than usual?

Smoothing her dress, Mathilde touched his shoulder. "Godfrey, my love," she said, "I've been looking all over for you. It seems we have a situation."

"A situation?" But what could touch them out here in his Fortress of Solitude, that impregnable Floating Island shaped like a woman's breast?

Rodrigue was leaning in, eavesdropping. And when he'd retreated, she said to Godfrey in a whisper, "It seems some of the girls have gotten out of their cages."

Well, put them back.

That was his initial reaction to what should not have been a four-alarm fire. He had people he paid to deal with situations like this, and they were good people, or anyway, good at what they did. He kept former CIA and Blackwater guys experienced in Black Ops on payroll—dudes who'd spent time at Guantanamo and Abu Ghraib—so he should not have to worry about quelling an insurrection of teenaged girls, most of whom came from broken homes and trailer parks in places like Florida and were jailbait and runaways, anyway.

Still, he felt a nagging sense of worry as he rejoined his guests as the first course was served.

"How do you like the ceviche?" He grinned. Rodrigue was in earshot, and he wanted the guy to hear this, how little his refined palate mattered.

"Delightful," said one guest, a former head of state.

"Briny," said another—someone commonly referred to as a thought-leader: taught at Harvard or Yale or someplace—smacking his lips.

"It's an old French recipe," Godfrey said, winking at Mathilde down the length of the table. "I've begged, but our chef won't tell me the secret."

Rodrigue had steam coming out of his ears. But it was all in good fun, and Godfrey was enjoying winding the guy up, or taking the piss, as that British prince would've said. And how apropos!

And 400 euros was chump change, the kind of money Godfrey made or lost in a fraction of a second on the global markets. Amazing to think an entire village might subsist on that kind of money for several years in parts of Africa and the Global South.

"Yes," the prince said, "briny. Quite a subtle bouquet if I do say so myself. Reminds me of something I once had in the Falklands."

At a noise from the hall, Mathilde turned her head, a look of concern on her face. Godfrey's hackles rose. But when he stood, she signaled to him that he should stay.

"I'll take care of this." And she folded her napkin, dropped it beside her plate, and left the room, again a faint sound of screaming from belowdecks as the door opened, everyone around that table doing their level best to ignore it.

Watching her leave, Godfrey was seized with the desire to rub one out. It wasn't natural. At 37 she was long past prime child-bearing age, and he did like them young, as even the sitting American President knew. But the sight of that middle-aged rump rolling under her dress excited him.

Or perhaps it was her power, the vicious things he'd seen her do, utterly unconscionable, at least if you were a normal person, which they were not, being above the laws of God and man.

Or maybe it was the power he held over her, power (as someone once said) being the ultimate aphrodisiac, in whatever direction it flowed.

"Do you mind if I masturbate?" he said to the dignitary sitting to his left.

One thing he'd found early on when working for the CIA, back in the early 80s when he'd begun to play the markets, Reagan and Thatcher making it easy for guys like him to make a killing— if they thought you had money, they would let you get away with anything.

The woman blushed. She'd been Secretary of State or something. He couldn't keep them straight, all the jerkoffs and suck-ups who dined at his table, who'd have let him fart in their dinner, if he asked nicely. But she said she didn't mind.

"Thank you."

When he'd finished, he cleaned himself with a napkin. Usually, he saved his ejaculations and froze them, intending to donate them for posterity, since future generations of scientists would study what he'd accomplished, and he didn't want to waste his sperm. But thanks to that macrobiotic diet, that fitness regime, and a steady regimen of underage pussy, he had the sex drive of a man half his age, so he had the spunk to spare.

And just in time for the main course.

But where had Rodrigue gotten to? Here were those beef wellingtons, and no, you didn't want to know what was in the brown sauce and not in the red sauce, either, but the grand saucier, the French bastard, had disappeared.

"Wellingtons?" the British prince said, "I do say. A devilish choice, old boy. Reminds me of my time at Eton."

Preoccupied as he was with the whereabouts of his chef and his second, Mathilde, Godfrey could've shot the pompous twat in the head. He might've catalogued the proclivities of each of his guests, told you which ones liked to wear diapers, which ones enjoyed being shat upon by schoolboys, and which ones wanted to be fondled by their mothers, and he had the videotapes to prove it. But sometimes all that power bored him to tears, and he could've walked any of those dolts onto the deck, drilled a hole in their foreheads, and skull-fucked them to death, just for a little variety, a little spice. Hell, for something to do.

"Tell me," he said, interrupting the people next to him, a couple of prattling Oxford dons, "what about the etymology of the word *fanny*? I just think it's so fascinating how on my side of the pond, it means the rear hole, but on your side of the water, it means the front hole."

Maybe he saw it then, a look of disbelief on those professors' faces, as if they were shocked at a stupid student. They'd been talking about Homer, and wasn't Ancient Greece a blueprint for what he was doing here, except of course he didn't fuck boys?

"Fanny?" The prince was swirling Beaujolais in his glass. It was a fine vintage, 1867, perfumed with what they didn't know was Mathilde's menstrual blood, which gave it a certain earthiness, or so they'd all agreed. Godfrey thought he saw that same look of disbelief on the prince's face.

"I just think it's so interesting how in America, it means the butt, the thing you sit on—" Godfrey was pointing at his chair—"but in your country, it means the pussy, the thing you fuck."

And he made a thrusting motion.

"Pussy?" the prince said.

"You know." Godfrey giggled. He pointed at his own crotch. "The snatch. The tuna taco. The place we all came from and where we're all trying to get back to, cock first."

"Yes." Swilling Beaujolais, the prince couldn't keep from making a sour face. Considering what Godfrey had on him, the man should watch himself. "Quite."

"Don't you think that tells us something about the psychology of the English," Godfrey said.

He felt as though he were about to make a profound argument. Yes, he was stumbling upon the very doorstep of profundity, tripping over the thing itself. That professor pursed her lips, and she might've been considering this point. She was on the verge of agreement, as was that clown from MIT, or maybe Harvard, whatever—Godfrey had likely funded her entire department or anyway a research project or three—but Mathilde burst into the room.

"Godfrey," she said, crooking a finger. "Kitchen. Now."

"Liquor in the front," he said, rising from his chair, "poker in the rear." And God, it was good to play a crucial role in the intellectual life of his Age. When the history of this time was written, they would remember him. "If you'll excuse me."

And he followed Mathilde through those swinging doors.

The kitchen was in disarray, stockpots bubbling over on the stove, an odor of burnt garlic wafting from the industrial-sized oven. Rodrigue had left the remains of what looked like a suckling pig under the broiler, which was set to a high flame. Across the room, under a white light, the desserts had been plated, tit-shaped meringues floating on plates of crème anglaise, floating islands in the image of the Floating Island itself.

"What the hell is happening?" Godfrey said. "Where's Rodrigue? Do you think the thing with the fish—the fugu—was too much for him? I thought the French were more laissez-faire. I didn't think they had such an underdeveloped sense of humor."

He smacked his forehead. He detected a different scent, one of singed hair. But he couldn't place it, not at first.

"Godfrey," Mathilde said in a patient tone. "I need you to pay attention to me."

"You know those intellectuals," he said. "Those eggheads need someone to remind them that it's all about dick and pussy, you know, the old in-and-out."

And he grabbed Mathilde's hips and thrust.

"Godfrey." Mathilde was shaking his shoulders. "You're not listening."

"What did you say?" Godfrey said. "Did you want to bone?"

Thanks to the hormones he was taking, his refractory period was shorter than it had been when he was 17. He'd just choked the chicken, but he could go again. Maybe if he finished inside her, they might use that to flavor the anglaise. He hated to waste his sperm, especially since he was planning on fathering a super race with those girls in the hold, but it would be worth it, just a few dribbles, anyway—a single load—for fun.

Mathilde slapped his face, then doused him with a glass of cooking sherry.

"Godfrey," she said, shouting at him, "goddammit, you're not listening, and I need you to hear what I'm saying."

The smell coming from the oven was worse than burnt garlic, whatever was burning too large to be a mere roast or even a suckling pig, and he began to have his first inkling of what it might be.

Mathilde poured herself another glass of cooking wine, gulped it. That was out of character for her, so this must be an emergency.

"I believe we have solved the mystery," she said in a tone that was dryer even than the pinot grigio she was drinking, "of how the young ladies in the hold escaped their bonds of captivity and achieved liberation."

She was slurring, and her mouth curled around the word *liberation*, as though it were the foulest word in the language, like she'd bitten into a rotten langoustine and wanted to spit it out.

When he pulled out the tray under the broiler, there was the chef—Rodrigue—trussed with his wrists fastened behind his back, his mouth stuffed with what looked like an eggplant, his chef's whites seared to his back, his face frozen into an agonized rictus of death. Yet charred and blackened as the flesh around his eyes was, Godfrey recognized the man's beady, determined expression.

"God in Heaven," he said, covering his nose as he stepped back from the stove. Smoke billowed into the room. Now that he knew what it was, the smell was intolerable.

Not that he believed in God or Heaven, only in his own ingenuity and invention. But certain aspects of his upbringing—certain colloquialisms—were inescapable.

"Don't blame this on God." Mathilde was gulping a third glass of wine, leaning against the cutting board. "No, the error here lies entirely with us, my dear, with you and me. For I believe it was a strategic mistake on our part, employing a chef with a weakness for underage snatch and giving him the run of the place when we have a hold full of teenage girls on this craft."

"You mean he let them out?" A cold feeling of betrayal sank through Godfrey's guts, along with a deeper certainty, a subterranean, as yet unnamable fear, as he took her meaning. "After all we did for him, paying off that judge, sneaking him out of the country, he betrayed us?"

He was, in a word, flabbergasted.

"Seems so, yes." Still holding her glass, wobbling, Mathilde gestured at Rodrigue's thigh, where the flesh had been carved away, sliced right down to the hipbone, which gleamed white under the kitchen lights. "I hope you didn't eat too much of the roast, dear."

He hadn't. He knew better than to eat anything produced in his own kitchen, not even a peanut butter and jelly sandwich, not unless he'd seen it made with his own eyes or better yet prepared it with his own two hands. Still, Godfrey barely made it to the sink in time to empty his guts into the basin.

Beneath him, the Floating Island pitched and rolled, the screams from the girls belowdecks louder.

Except those screams were no longer cries of terror but had coalesced into something else, into shrill, implacable cries of rage.

And make no mistake, they were coming for him.

As many times as they'd discussed this, he was prepared. He had a way out, those cyanide capsules he kept in a secret compartment in the heel of his shoe, for one, not to mention the lethal overdose of fentanyl in a syringe in the hollowed-out copy of *The Prince* on his bedside table. And whatever those bloodthirsty bitches had done to Rodrigue, they still had to make it through the ex-Blackwater and the ex-Agency guys Godfrey had hired as his security apparatus.

Or did they?

"What about Jones?" he said. "Or Jonas? Whatever the hell his name is."

He could never keep all those square-jawed, crewcut dudes straight. Anyway, the ex-Iraq and Afghanistan vet who was head of the security detail, a former Navy SEAL, a sharpshooter, a man versed in extraordinary rendition. Guy had practically written the book on waterboarding.

"Gone." Mathilde was pouting. She'd had work done, undetectable as it was. They shared a plastic surgeon, and he was one of the best in the world, had honed his skills working on Nazi war criminals in Brazil and Argentina. But it was too late for that. In the half-light in the kitchen, her face looked craggy, her cheeks drooping.

"Gone?" Godfrey spit into the sink. "What do you mean gone?"

Prepared as he was, he hadn't imagined it going down like this. Those video recordings he had of world leaders in compromising positions weren't going to help him now. After all, he might've blackmailed a former President, a politician, even a department chair at an Ivy, the head of a multinational, or a prominent tech bro, but what hold could he have over people who he'd robbed of everything? How could he threaten people he'd humiliated so badly that they were scarcely more than animals in cages, with nothing left to lose?

"I mean they're gone," Mathilde said. "They took the helicopter. Those that didn't get away were—how shall I say this?" She gulped wine, but she was calmer, more in control than a moment ago. "Subdued. Some of them were subdued in a manner that would make what happened to our dear chef here seem a mercy."

And she gestured with her glass at Rodrigue, whose remains were smoking under the broiler.

"They took the helicopter?" Godfrey said, dread clawing at his intestines, a slow understanding dawning on him of just how fucked they were.

"They took the helicopter," Mathilde said. "Indeed."

"What about the lifeboats, the submarine?"

But she was shaking her head. Was she enjoying their—his—predicament?

"Took those too, I'm afraid."

He leaned closer, speaking in a whisper. "What about the top-secret escape pod?"

He'd long ago had installed in the depths of the island a craft that fit two and that could be launched toward the mainland in direst emergency such as this, parachuting them to safety in the Florida panhandle, where Godfrey had a bunker and several local politicians on the payroll.

If all else failed, when the shit hit the fan, they were going to the panhandle, to Florida's 1st Congressional District.

Only he and Mathilde had known about it—and by necessity, whoever was acting head of security.

But again, Mathilde was shaking her head.

"Gone," she whispered. "Gone, gone, gone."

"Then how are we supposed to get off this island," he said, "this giant, floating tit?"

Mathilde was making a face, sucking her cheeks, like she was disappointed in him. And maybe he was losing his cool. Leaning against the cutting board with her hip cocked, in her sequined dress, holding her glass, Mathilde might have been entertaining guests at a cocktail party. But he recognized in her posture the attitude of a woman resigned to disaster, like they were on the Titanic drifting toward that iceberg.

"My best guess," she said, "is that we're 170 miles from the mainland. So, unless you're prepared to swim, I'd say we're not supposed to get off of it. I'd say we're not going anywhere."

"Impossible," Godfrey whispered.

And he said it again.

But he knew that it was true.

His guts roiling like the vast ocean they were floating upon, Godfrey bent to the sink, once more heaved up what remained of his lunch, then rinsed his mouth, and spit.

He snuck a glance at Rodrigue. What they had stuffed in the man's mouth was not in fact an eggplant, but the man's own once-prodigious member.

And no, those were not eggs they'd stuffed in there with it but the man's testicles, those ropy gonads unraveling like balls of yarn.

A heat blister on the man's thigh popped, a greasy wisp of smoke billowing up into the hoods above the oven. Godfrey heaved, but however he retched, he had nothing left to bring up. "Pull yourself together," he whispered to himself. "Pull yourself together, man."

And he slapped some cold water on his face, rinsed the aftertaste of vomit from his mouth, and stood. Stiff upper lip and all that. Or so that British prince would say.

Mathilde was crying.

"You never loved me," she said, "did you? You never cared one whit for me, you rotten, selfish son of a bitch."

And she hurled the glass at him. It shattered on the broiler, dousing Rodrigue's form in pinot grigio, basting him.

Good God, not this.

"You and your rotten stable of filthy underage bitches," she said.

"Now, now," Godfrey said. "I don't think this is the time, dear."

And he went to her, but she shoved him away.

Did he need to remind her that she had helped him to recruit that harem, he said, that she'd had her way with nearly as many of those girls as he had?

Did he need to remind her of the filthy, unconscionable things she'd done, and done enthusiastically, as his accomplice every step of the way?

Did he need to remind her of how she'd earned, then abused their trust, an older woman, a maternal figure offering poor young girls from broken homes cold, hard cash for a massage for her husband, for a few photographs?

Did he really need to remind her, he said, of the tiger shark?

"Don't touch me," she said, clawing his face. "It was your idea, all of it. Monster."

Godfrey slapped her, and she fell away, sobbing, holding her cheek.

When he touched his face, blood was on his hand.

"The way I recall things happening," Godfrey said, "you helped me break most of those young fillies in."

"What else was I supposed to do, Daddy?" she said, mascara streaking her face. "I thought that was the only way you would love me."

"Don't start with that psychobabble," he said.

The first impact came, the kitchen door shuddering on its hinges.

The place was on fire, an orange glow surrounding the door in its frame.

The impact came again, but the deadbolt held, for now.

"What we've accomplished here is the pinnacle of Western civilization," Godfrey said. "We'll be remembered. We'll be written about in the history books like the Greeks and the ancient Roman kings. You can't let it be torn down by something as stupid as petty jealousy."

And he grabbed her and held her, stroking her hair.

For though this could end in only one way, he was clinging to life, to the hope they would escape their fate. And failing that, at least he had that cyanide capsule in his shoe, which would spare him from meeting an end like Rodrigue's.

Yes, he could still take the long goodbye and avoid the pain and the indignity of either prison or—more likely—being unmanned and cooked alive.

No way he would make it back to his bedroom and the comfort of that fentanyl, his beloved Machiavelli, and his collection of Ayn Rand, not unless he went through that burning doorway.

And no way was he doing that.

"You son of a bitch." Mathilde was whispering into his chest. She was cooing. "You're a filthy, rotten coward, Godfrey. You're an idiot, and everyone at that table thinks so. They only pretend to take your stupid ideas seriously because you have money."

And she stomped on his foot, breaking his toe with her heel.

And whatever she'd intended, she accomplished the one thing that might still destroy him, for he heard a click as the compartment in the heel of his shoe opened, and when he lifted his foot, that cyanide capsule—his salvation—rolled across the floor toward the oven, where it disappeared beneath the broiler pan with the chef's body.

For a horrid second, as if in slow motion, he saw himself leaping after it—saw himself diving under the broiler tray and scooping the pill up from under the oven before it rolled down the drain in the floor—but that was mere delusion, for though he threw himself after the pill, though he crawled under the broiler tray, the heat from the oven singeing the hairs on his head and scorching his back, the pill escaped his grasp.

It teetered on the edge of the drain. Then with his own finger, he bumped it, and it was gone, dropping into the blackness where they flushed their waste, the legacy of all he'd done, all the pain and the suffering and the bodily fluids they'd flushed away for the betterment of civilization.

When the door went, he would be waiting for them, and history would vindicate him. For hadn't he done what anyone would have done, given his circumstances? And hadn't he achieved those by dint of his superiority, etched in his genes? And weren't they expendable, all those who'd suffered, who he'd fucked and fucked over, like the peasants whose bones lay underneath the roads the Russian tzars had built? For throughout human history, hadn't there always been winners and losers?

When they dragged him out by the legs, he would beg for mercy, but there would be none.

Toiler Cartoon Dept., Columbus Dispatch, ~1920

"But getting together with her in the real world didn't seem to be Devon's intention. He just wanted to be photographed with her."

Schicksal (The German Word for Destiny)

Steven-Elliot Altman

I don't think there's a man on Earth with a working cock, myself included—and few women for that matter—who would disagree with *Vogue*, *Elle*, and *Cosmo* that Natalia Petrova was one of the world's hottest models. At twenty-one she'd appeared out of nowhere; now twenty-six, she had the world by the balls. Her flawless skin and lucrative amber eyes had the glamor hounds in a lather. But one man was willing to spend a sizeable portion of his inherited fortune to be with her, at least on film.

Devon Blaylock had been quite the Casanova back in the day—handsome, filthy rich, private jets, residences all over Europe. He broke a lot of hearts. Then he dropped out of sight. Rumor had it he joined a twelve-step program and lived most of the year in a big house on a dead-end street off a secluded bluff in Malibu, California. Whatever the facts, for all practical purposes the thirty-two-year-old billionaire was now a recluse who went out of his way to avoid meeting anyone.

Then Blaylock ran an online contest—anonymously, of course—to reconstruct a photo of a girl in a bikini on a blanket at the beach, her back to the camera, cuddling her dog, a Dalmatian.

I was living in my car, typically parked somewhere non-permit along the canals of Venice Beach, aspiring to be a published writer—if you haven't done it by thirty, you're probably fucked; I had two years left and a desktop littered with half-finished literary works-in-progress. I took pictures to pay the bills. The contest prize was a thousand dollars, a fortune to me at the time. I recognized Zuma Beach in Malibu straight off, and knew a girl roughly the same proportions as the model, who happened to own a white Labrador. I had all the necessary software and plug-ins I'd need to "spot" the dog. So, I entered the contest, on a lark.

"You know why you won?" Blaylock asked me in that steel British accent, seated across from me at the desk in his Malibu study. "You got the lighting bang-on. Sun's in just the right place. Took patience."

I swiveled from eyeing the breathtaking view of the coast to the large framed print on the wall behind Blaylock: Natalia Petrova exiting a limo, signature moose-eared tongue-out gesture aimed at a throng of paparazzi. *Why is that there?* I wondered.

"I've had you checked out," Blaylock continued, and paused to let it sink in. "I'm offering you a full-time job as a photographer on a pet project."

"I'm afraid I can't accept a full-time position, Mr. Blaylock," I responded.

Then he mentioned the job included use of his guest house, state-of-the-art equipment, and a sum large enough to put all my personal projects on hold for as long as he liked.

"One last question," he said as we signed our NDA. "Did you sleep with her?"

I presumed he meant the model in my photo reconstruction. Not that it was any of his business. This job would enable me to ease my guilt by replacing the bad check I'd given her.

"No," I said, stepping to the study door.

"Right. In any case, you're forbidden to have sex with Miss Petrova. Not that I could stop either of you. But understand, it would immediately terminate your employment."

As if, I thought, and closed the door behind me.

❖

The fact is, Devon Blaylock could easily have met and possibly wooed Natalia Petrova. In addition to his great wealth, he was fit, well-mannered, and handsome, with slick blond hair and piercing blue eyes, and she was rumored to be single after a public breakup with her last, Oscar-winning boyfriend. But getting together with her in the real world didn't seem to be Devon's intention. He just wanted to be photographed with her.

Well, not *with her*, exactly. My job was to include him in existing photos of her as if he'd been present at the shoot. He wouldn't say why, but I figured the reason would become evident. Maybe he didn't care who she really was, reality being the odds-on favorite to demolish fantasy. My initial assignment was to alter her debut spread in *Sports Illustrated*.

Devon handed me a pristine copy of the magazine. I flipped it open to the centerfold, taken in Italy—a waifish, bronze Petrova lying on the sand in a swimsuit that left little to the imagination. Haunted eyes. Rose petal lips. Breasts like ripe fruit. I'd seen the photo online; the first image of her I'd ever beheld, arousing me at a mere glance. It had the same effect now.

Devon wasn't interested in me simply manipulating the photo digitally to include him. No. I had to photograph him on location then "marry" his image with Petrova's. The picture had no blank beach around her in which to add him and continue any true background perspective. A wider shot was needed, and the finished reconstruction had to be seamless.

Twenty-four hours later, camera in hand, I was still fighting jetlag on that same Italian beach, with Devon due any moment from our hotel. I had hired two local assistants online, a brother and sister in their twenties who spoke decent English. Devon gave me several hundred Euros which I handed to the sister, instructing her to pay any beachgoers—quite nicely, thank you—to move out of the perimeter of our shoot.

Devon seemed pleased when he arrived, wearing a plush hotel robe. I showed him my tablet, on which I had lined up my best test shot.

"Unless you have something else in mind, I'm going for a mirror effect," I explained. "As if you were just offscreen, lying opposite her."

"You mean, as if it were originally one image? That we were shot together but I'd been cut out?"

"Precisely."

His face lit up, to my delight.

He removed his robe, revealing a toned, well-tanned body—benefits of a beach house and personal trainer. I shot at least two hundred photos of him. He took direction well and emanated a warm glow throughout, passion brimming his eyes, which surprised me. When I finished, he gave me an unexpected hug, then waded out into the warm current and swam while I packed the gear.

I worked on the photo in Devon's Malibu guesthouse for days, barely sleeping, until it was just right: Natalia on the left in her *Sports Illustrated* glory, a smiling Devon lying off to her right in a matching pose, the Amalfi coastline sprawling beyond them.

I stood anxiously the next morning in Devon's study, tablet in hand, as he stared blankly at the eight-by-ten glossy for several long moments. I was pretty sure it was perfect. But still . . .

At last he spoke.

"May I see the runners-up?"

Wary now, I showed him the best alternate shots, leaning in and scrolling through the tablet until he stopped me.

"You're right," he said. "This is the one. Delete the rest and have it blown up as far as it can go. I'll let you know our next location tomorrow."

In my excitement I left my tablet behind. I was about to knock when I heard him moan. Placing an ear to the door, I heard the unmistakable sounds of frenzied masturbation. I listened until he came, reveling in this compliment to my work.

Three months later, photographs of Devon's fairytale romance with Natalia filled the walls of the Malibu house.

One of my favorites, now hanging above the living room fireplace, is the *Madame Figaro* recreation, a picnic scene on the Eiffel Tower. Natalia stands at the base of the steeple, high over the plaza. She's sucking a ripe strawberry held in her manicured fingers, her back arched against the steel girders, head tilted backward to jut her breasts, the steeple soaring above her. Shot from the stairwell below, the angle is basically straight up her skirt, featuring the cleft of her crotch—to sell the bright leggings and matching panties clinging tightly to her soft, oiled skin.

Devon paid a hefty six figures to have the tower closed to the public; he seemed to get off on approving the bank transfer, standing in his lavender robe, phone in hand, on the balcony of his luxurious Paris apartment.

I tried conceptualizing the main interaction between Devon and Natalia without the crotch spread revealed, but there was no getting around it. I needed to position Devon to become the object of Natalia's raw sexuality. I settled on standing him with his back to the rail, as far from her as possible, with sun-soaked Paris glistening beyond them. In his hand I placed a large, ripe strawberry twin to hers, telling him to bite into it with abandon, imagining it was her pussy, allowing the juice to drizzle down. We went through three packs of strawberries. Juice streamed across Devon's lips, chin, and cheeks, dampening his dark Armani jacket and leaving an ever-spreading bright red stain on his white shirt and sleeve cuffs. I pulled in tight, thrusting Devon into focus, usurping Natalia's passion.

The end result is the suggestion that she is symbolically taking his manhood tenderly in her mouth, while his biting into the strawberry—one gleaming white eyetooth piercing the skin, the curve of his engorged tongue enveloping the cleft of the fruit, the juice spraying against his expensive suit, his face contorted in ecstasy, free hand gripping the rail to steady himself, hips poised to grind the open air between them—is him ravaging her.

Confident I had what I needed, I handed him a wet towel to clean his hands before offering him my tablet to preview the photos, then watched him scroll gleefully as I packed up.

❖

Natalia's editorial spread in *Paper* was her first topless photo in print. While people on benches watch her, Natalia lies on her back in a huge bed, blown-out hair spilling over the edge to one side, arms crossed over her bare breasts, hands resting flat on her shoulders—more a protective gesture than for concealment, since both erect nipples are visible. A cropped leather miniskirt clings to her waist above fishnet stockings trailing down into stilettos. Her high-set, alabaster cheeks and blood red lips contrast like a China doll's as she gazes wantonly at the opposite side of the bed with just a hint of surprise. I needed Devon to be that surprise.

The shoot's location, a Berlin club notorious for casual debauchery, was one of Devon's old haunts. He hired two former associates, both drop-dead-gorgeous German models, to assist us: Nina, a full-figured platinum blonde, and Phoebe, a slender jet-black brunette. I was no longer surprised by how well they spoke English in the car from Devon's posh West-Berlin flat, or when Devon responded in fluent German. Both wore S&M leather, to fit in with the club's dress code. (Many called it an "undress code," since nudity was encouraged—the fewer clothes the better.) Devon was wearing a latex tuxedo.

LIFE IS A CIRCUS proclaimed the sign posted outside the club. We arrived to find a line snaking around the block. A young man in shiny red leather chaps, bare chest and arms covered with tattoos, was waiting for us at the entrance beside the bouncers, who were in the process of turning away a tourist couple in parkas and jeans.

"Welcome to KitKat," the young man said. "I'm Kristof, the club's photographer."

"We spoke on the phone," Devon said.

"Yes. Thank you for making the deposit. Can I have the camera, please?"

Cameras and mobile phones are forbidden on the premises. Devon had hired Kristof to accompany us as staff photographer and turn a blind eye while I worked; though it had to be done *just so*, as German politics demanded.

He ushered us through the swinging doors, past the cashier in a French maid's outfit, into a reception area where three young women at a long wooden bar collected customers' phones, and anything else they wished to store, stowing them in cubbyholes and handing back retrieval tickets. I was surprised to see Nina and Phoebe strip off their jackets and hand them to check-in.

Nina's torso was fully covered by colorful tattoos, except for her large, pale breasts. Phoebe's tiny nipples were pierced with rings. They didn't seem to mind my staring. Devon just smiled as he removed his jacket to carry with him. I did the same with my latex sport coat.

Phoebe, noting me looking at a sign in German above the entrance to the club proper, translated: "'Magic Theater. Admission not for everyone. Only for crazy people. Admission costs the mind!' It's a quote from Hermann Hesse's *Steppenwolf*."

We followed Kristof past vintage cigarette vending machines on our left, and a candy store to our right that displayed lollipops, wax lips, and penis-shaped gummies.

We were now in a tiki-themed area with a swimming pool big enough for at least thirty people, surrounded by eight small cabanas, all open to the pool, where couples sat on couches, making out or more. I watched a nude young man run, leap onto a narrow swing suspended from the ceiling by ropes, and fling himself into the pool, the huge splash dousing nearby couples.

"In addition to nudity, KitKat encourages sexual activity, anywhere and everywhere in the club guests wish to indulge themselves," Kristof explained. "But it must at all times be voluntary and consensual. Understood?"

"Yes," I responded.

A painting of a demon with glowing eyes above the main dance hall entrance seemed to welcome us, while a marble statue of an angel, wings outstretched, looked the other way. A wave of live techno music washed over us as we entered. Hundreds of half-nude clubbers, fists in the air, danced with abandon to the DJ's ministrations.

Kristof led us along the perimeter of the dance floor, a large industrial-looking space lit by strobe lights, with two huge disco balls and a half-dozen stripper poles, the walls lined with Day-Glo paintings depicting every conceivable sex act. Vintage German porn played in a loop on two large, mounted video screens projecting downward. I saw a lot of finger-banging, and a girl giving a man a blowjob on the dance floor, his leather pants around his ankles. In one corner, a burly Viking flogged a woman bent over a chair, reddening her bare bottom with welts. In a cage beside the DJ booth, a man wearing a police uniform demonstrated how to properly bind together a slender blonde's arms with knotted rope.

"Down these stairs you'll see hardcore sex play," Kristof said, leading the way.

As if on cue, I smelled the thick, unmistakable scent of semen and heard ecstatic moans. Next we saw people riding motorized sex toys. A gynecologist's chair. Dispensers for lubricant.   Two men were penetrating a woman on a swing at both ends, her hands and legs bound. I locked eyes with her as we passed, feeling a thrill. Her glazed look told me she enjoyed it. If anyone in our group was disturbed, they didn't show it.

Finally, we arrived at the site of Natalia's shoot, a large, red, rectangular room with a chessboard floor. A bright, colorfully lit bar area was full but not crowded like the dance hall, and there in the opposite corner was the bed, occupied by several people chilling, cuddling, or screwing, while spectators watched from the benches.

Devon, the ladies, and I ambled over to the triangular bar staffed by tenders wearing only see-through netting. I watched Phoebe discreetly hand Nina a pill that she chased with a shot of Jaeger Meister. She offered me one too.

"Save it for later," I said. "I have enough distractions in here already."

Nina turned to me to chat, about what I don't remember, my attention being caught by Phoebe and Devon conversing intensely in German.

Kristof interrupted us. "The show in the main hall is about to start," he said. "It should help clear this room." He handed me my camera. "I'll check on you later."

With a wink he was gone. Everyone on the bed got up and left too, except one heavyset couple fucking. It was hard to take our eyes off them. We had no choice but to wait patiently until they were done, whereupon they left.

Devon came out of the restroom dressed in his latex tuxedo, as I lined up the shot. I'd have to keep the original background crowd from the *Paper* spread. I had no idea how I was going to incorporate him. I marked a spot with two round stickers.

"Those are Natalia's eyes," I told Devon. "Remember to keep your eyes set on them."

I must have shot three hundred photos, improvising poses as we proceeded. Nina and Phoebe kept clubbers from approaching the bed, making out with strangers if necessary.

At last, I was satisfied I'd gotten as much as I could from Devon. Phoebe once again offered me whatever those pills were. Something told me to say no. Devon and Nina readily accepted. Drinks flowed, techno music pounded, and some toad in the restroom, standing eager by the urinal trough, asked me if I wanted to pee in his mouth. I told him I'd think about it.

One thing led to another and Devon and the ladies ended up having sex in the bed. I held back, resisting the urge to use my camera, sure they wouldn't notice if I did, they were so into each other. Devon said nothing about it when we finally awoke in his immaculate apartment the next evening, and it wasn't my place to bring it up.

Nina and Phoebe had crashed in the second guest room. As they were preparing to leave, I took Phoebe aside and asked, "What were you and Devon talking about in German by the bar?"

"He told me why you were making this photo," she said. "The supermodel. I told him she could be his *Schicksal*. How to say in English—his *destiny*. You're helping him to manifest her."

If the twelve-step rumors were true, was Devon feeling guilty over slipping? Or did he interpret it as cheating on Natalia? I wasn't about to ask him. We barely spoke on the plane. He declined to go through the photos on my tablet, saying he would wait until I made my selection.

I liked three pictures equally but couldn't choose one. Back home, around midnight, it finally clicked. Why not use them all—one Devon mounting the bed, one kneeling nude on the floor in the foreground, one lying opposite Natalia—all three staring back at her, the multiple Devons magnifying his adoration to tell a larger story. Genius, if you ask me.

I stood behind Devon at breakfast, peering over his shoulder as he gazed and gazed at the final image on my laptop. Finally, he spoke.

"I hate it."

"Why?" I nearly sputtered.

His face contorted.

I realized it challenged his fantasy.

"How stupid of me. I'll have a second go ready by lunchtime."

"Delete it," he demanded.

I dragged the folder to Trash, thinking, *Doesn't he realize I save copies of everything to the cloud?*

The tension drained from Devon's shoulders. But something had changed. Something was wrong. For a moment he'd seemed almost—*homicidal.*

"I look forward to seeing your second go. Can you pass the salt?"

❖

My next assignment was a recreation from an unpublished set of photos shot on 35mm film, requiring me to send out the negatives to be developed and digitized. Devon didn't say how they came into his possession.

A young, pre-famous Natalia sporting a perfect tan, dirty blonde locks hanging down to her ass, in Daisy Duke cutoffs and a gingham bikini top. I thought of the photo of the girl on a beach that started me on this journey. *Could she be . . .? No.* But the location looked awfully familiar. I walked down the private wooden stairwell to assure myself I wasn't imagining things.

I wasn't. The photos had been shot at the bluff, in direct view of Devon's house. *Could this be where the obsession started? Was he looking down from his balcony, saw a pretty girl, and fell in love?*

Devon was out for the day. I was alone on the beach, camera on a tripod, running test shots, measuring the light to get the perfect time of day. I was hot as hell and sweating. I took a break to have a dip. When I came back to the rig, I dug through my camera bag to find sunblock, squeezed some into my hands, applied it to my face and shoulders, then studied a shot I liked: Natalia leaning back against a smooth rock set into the bluff in the high grass—topless, blonde locks tastefully concealing her breasts except for the sensual cleft, legs spread at just the right vulnerable angle in her loose-fitting jean shorts.

I flipped to another photo: Natalia against the rock with her firm, untanned left breast exposed, legs spread farther apart, a come-hither look on her face. I imagined the photographer doing just that. Then I imagined it was me, pressing my body against hers, one hand clutching that firm exposed breast, pinching the nipple hard, the other hand pressed between her legs, probing her wet warmth through the crotch of her shorts . . .

A sudden urge seized me. I looked around the empty beach. I was still alone. I fished in my bag, found the remote cable, attached it to the camera, and took the photo with me across the hot sand, past the grass to the rock, to use as my guide.

◈

I lay exhausted on the guest house couch, watching dawn break through the window with slitted eyes. A bottle of Jaeger and skull-shaped shot glass on the coffee table beside my laptop. Onscreen, yours truly having sex with young Natalia Petrova against a smooth rock set into the bluff in the high grass of Malibu beach. The image was finished but I was too tired, or too drunk, to cum. Maybe both.

I startled awake in motion, Devon's nails biting into my skin as he wrenched me by the shirt collar over the back of the couch and slammed me against the floor. I punched him hard in the face. He returned the favor a half dozen times before I wriggled back onto my feet. We swung back and forth at each other, grunting, shouting, knocking a vase from a table and flipping the couch, sending my laptop, the bottle, and glass flying.

The bottle shattered. David grasped the remains by the neck and held the jagged edge to my throat. Murder in his eyes.

I raised my hands in surrender, shouting, "It's not real, man!"

He paused, then dropped the bottle and kicked me hard in the testicles with his pointed Oxford shoe. Agony. I dropped to the floor gasping, too incapacitated to stop him as he moved past the upturned couch, grabbed the laptop and tablet, and stepped to the door.

"You're fired," he said. "I needn't remind you that everything on these machines belongs to me. And since you breached the contract, I'll keep them. Leave your keys with my secretary and get out."

He slammed the door behind him.

In time, the pain subsided to a dull ache. With some effort I righted the couch and sank down on it. I was pissed off. I'd broken the rules in his fantasy world and he'd assaulted me. Threatened my life. If he was going to make me the bad guy, I'd show him how it was done.

I called in a favor from an old buddy who owned an art gallery at Bergamot Station, the trendy complex in Santa Monica. The invite had gone out that morning to everyone who mattered in Hollywood—celebrities, agents, press.

You are cordially invited to attend
THE DREAM COUPLE
a photographic chronicle of
the covert, lurid, whirlwind romance between
Supermodel Natalia Petrova
and
reclusive billionaire arts patron
Devon Blaylock

Now the exhibit was set to begin. The catering was prepped, security standing by.

I paced nervously outside the gallery.

"James, there you are!"

Constance, the model for the photo that won me my job, was my date for the event, a welcome distraction strolling toward me in a beautiful designer gown. She rose on her toes to kiss my cheek.

"You're early," I said. "You look lovely."

"Thanks," she said, twirling to reveal her backless dress. "And thanks for the check. You didn't have to double it."

"I wanted to make up for the one that bounced."

I removed my sunglasses.

"What happened to your eye? Were you in a fight?"

"It's nothing," I said.

"I'm so excited to see your work. I had no idea Blaylock was dating Petrova. Will they be here?"

"Your guess is as good as mine."

Over her shoulder, I recognized Devon's car pulling into the lot. *Speak of the devil.*

"Why don't you go in and I'll join you soon?" I suggested.

Constance headed inside. I watched Devon get out of the car, dressed in one of his limited-edition Armani suits. I tipped my chin to the head security guard; he inclined his head slightly in acknowledgment.

"I see I left an impression," Devon said, indicating my eye.

"It's part of the exhibit," I responded.

"You know, if what's in there is what I suspect I'll sue you out of existence." It wasn't a question.

I spread my arms. "Your money paid for it, Devon. The pictures aren't for sale."

"It's about the publicity then? The kind you can't buy, so you steal it from those around you? Is it vengeance? Or both?"

I didn't answer. He didn't expect me to.

"Did you invite her?"

"Did you want me to?"

Gritting his teeth, he pushed past me into the gallery.

"Follow him," I told the guard. "Make sure he doesn't slash anything."

I should be so lucky.

A throng of guests approached the gallery; it was time for me to go in. I couldn't wait to see Devon's reaction to the exhibit.

All of the images were blown up to max capacity and hung in the order they'd been shot. I found Devon brooding over the picture of him and Natalia on the Amalfi Coast. I stood behind him at a discreet distance, unsure if he was aware of my presence. Guests continued to arrive, filling the gallery.

I shadowed Devon, observing his reactions as he moved slowly through the thirty-nine oversized photos comprising the sum of their relationship—literally—and of ours as well. The *Paper* redo hung in a side room, covering an entire twelve-by-twenty-foot wall. A few other guests considered the shot beside Devon.

Satisfied, I walked off to find Constance.

"It seems to be going splendidly," she said as we stood at the bar.

People crowded about, gawking and taking pictures of my recreations of other people's pictures. Before long, their images would be shared on social media, and Natalia Petrova would see them, eventually. Vengeance would be mine.

Constance clutched my arm, interrupting my musings.

"Is that her?" she asked.

I followed her gaze to the gallery's front door. This I had truly not expected.

Natalia was alone, dressed simply, hair pulled back tightly behind big sunglasses. But I'd have recognized her anywhere.

"You'll introduce me, won't you?"

I downed my drink and took a deep breath.

"Come," I said, then, "Welcome to the show, Ms. Petrova," when we reached her.

Heads began turning as word spread. She removed her sunglasses with a gloved hand.

"Are you the one responsible?" she asked, clearly perturbed.

"I'm James, the photographer," I replied. "And this is Constance."

She offered each of us in turn her gloved hand. Curtly.

"Well, let's see it," she said.

Constance diplomatically excused herself to go to the ladies' room. I walked with Natalia around the gallery, watching her scrutinize each picture without comment. After studying the Eiffel Tower redo at length, she asked, "Why have you done this?"

"Maybe you should ask Devon," I answered.

"Mr. Blaylock is here?"

"I'll take you to him. But first I have a question, if you wouldn't mind."

"Ask it."

"I saw photos of you in Malibu when you were really young, and I was wondering—"

"If I was screwing the photographer?"

"No," I said. "I wondered if you'd already met Devon when those pictures were taken?"

"How could a poor immigrant kid ever meet a billionaire? Why do you ask?"

"The beach you were shot on is right below Devon's house."

"Oh my God, that's *his* house? I must have walked past it on that beach a hundred times. It's so beautiful. I remember looking up at it and thinking somehow, someday, I would live in that house."

Chills ran down my spine.

"Come with me," I said.

Devon was alone in the side room. He looked up from the bench in disbelief when we entered.

"Devon, I'd like you to meet Natalia Petrova."

She extended a gloved hand as I left.

I never saw either of them in person again. They both refused all interview requests. (I did too, saying only that the photographs spoke for themselves.) Natalia's reps announced she was taking a hiatus from modeling and she disappeared from public view. Eventually the scandal died down.

A year passed. At Constance's suggestion, she and I started a modeling agency. It was just taking off when I received a manila envelope from Devon. Inside was a letter voiding our Non-Disclosure Agreement. Also enclosed was a sonogram of a baby girl and, handwritten on the back, "*Thank you!*"

Schicksal, indeed—and I was now free to write about it.

My chest tightened with jealousy. Well, that was a surprise.

"The Condition of the Laboring Man at Pullman" Cartoon, ~1894

"On the one hand, there was everything he had spent his life building: business, status, family. On the other hand, the money."

Trust Me

Lin Morris

M r. Diamond rose from behind his wood and granite desk, hand extended to greet his guest.

"Welcome to Death, Incorporated, Mr. Smith," he said. "Tell me what brings you here." Diamond was aptly named: glowy and white, but with a hard sheen, most likely the result of brow lifts and Botox.

"My name isn't Smith, it's—"

"Bup-bup-bup," said Diamond, wagging a threatening finger. His jeweled ring glinted in the light. "Not relevant. Today you're Mr. Smith." He gestured to a sumptuously upholstered chair. "Assuming you decide to engage our services, of course." He might have winked; it was hard to tell, what with the tightly tucked cat eyes.

Smith took a seat, smoothed his jacket, and spent several seconds basking in the low hum of the central air, set to the perfect temperature. "Like I told you on the phone, I'm interested," he said. "So, who recommended me to you?"

"No names!" Diamond took a slow breath, recovered himself. "For obvious reasons, Mr. Smith, we don't discuss our other clients."

"Don't I have a right to know who to thank?"

"Whom."

"*Whom* to thank."

"Mr. Smith, I doubt you've thanked anyone in a very long time."

"True." He smiled and sat up a bit straighter.

"You've been vetted, let's leave it at that," Diamond said. "We don't offer our services to just anyone, trust me."

Smith frowned. "And why Smith?"

"Come again?"

"Why do you call me Smith?"

Diamond spread his lips into a huge, thin smile. With his stretched skin and black eyes, he looked vaguely reptilian. "We've found that when blending into a new identity, it's best to keep it simple."

"But Smith? Really? You couldn't come up with something more original?"

"Simple genetics, Smith," said Diamond. "No offense, but you don't look like a Washington, a Rodriguez, or a Chin, the other names in our roster. Smith suits you. Smith has—power." Diamond clenched his fist. His smooth face may have expressed awe. "Tell me what brings you here."

Thirty minutes later Smith had spilled the gory details—the certainty of indictments for what the Feds insisted on calling "embezzlement." All because the shareholders couldn't see why he, Smith, needed a little extra money atop his salary as the CEO of—but, of course, Diamond silenced him before he could say the company name, as though he didn't know who Smith was the minute he walked in. Why, when he inherited the company from his father, it was barely turning a profit. Now it was the most popular fast-food chain in the country. Nay, in the world!

More sophisticated people would instinctively understand the price of maintaining a certain standing in society; these things aren't cheap. Never mind the obvious, like the right schools for his children (even the one he suspected wasn't actually his) and the best clothes for his wife, the uni-monikered former fashion model Britnee (again, Diamond cut in with the enforced anonymity before Smith could give name to her). Not to mention alimony for the three wives before her. He'd earned that secret quarter-billion!

"And don't even get me started on the cost of having a private jet! For someone as busy as me, it's a necessity—who has time for ticket counters and TSA lines?"

Sure, the jet was technically for business, but with his schedule, who could begrudge him a little time for relaxation? He needed it at hand for quick jaunts to indulge in his favorite extreme sports, like hang-gliding over Lake Avandaro, Mexico; bungee jumping from Macau Tower in China; kayaking the Nile from Uganda; riding the New York City subway incognito during rush hour.

Diamond nodded. "These things are required for a man of your position. If paying the airplane's staff to be on permanent stand-by costs more than the combined annual household income of Montana, why is that *your* fault?"

"Exactly! It's all too much," Smith said. "Being me is *hard*." His voice cracked with such pubescent passion it might as well have acne.

"Of course it is," said Diamond, with a low purr.

"Poor people have no idea." Smith pulled a handkerchief from his breast pocket and dabbed at his eyes, taking care to avoid soiling the Prada logo.

"Smith!" Diamond's nostrils flared. "Be a man."

"Right. Sorry."

"Be the man who made your corporation what it is today!"

"Go on," said Smith. He hid his proud smile by picking a piece of lint from his trouser leg. "What is it you can do for me?"

"To be clear from the start: to the outside world, you will be dead. That means no contacting your family, no changing your mind."

Smith gnawed at his thumbnail, a new-ish habit brought on by the stress of simply being him.

"Still interested?"

On the one hand, there was everything he had spent his life building: business, status, family.

On the other hand, the money. All that money tucked away in Swiss banks, at his disposal. Finally his.

"What say you, Smith?"

For a moment, Britnee loomed in his mind. But when he thought of his wife, all he heard was the constant nagging: *you never take me anywhere good; why do you always have to take Viagra?; these aren't Louboutins!* What used to pass as alluring innocence had revealed itself to be plain old stupidity. Besides, ever since she'd turned twenty-six, the trophy was beginning to tarnish.

He was sixty and, until this past year, could have passed for forty. His mental stamina alone surpassed men half his age. Running a corporation took nerve. It was more bracing than white water rafting.

"Tick-tock, Smith."

And what did his children want, anyway, besides his money? Always one hand out for the newest whatever. They appreciated the free burgers and fries more than they appreciated him.

"I know a dozen men who would kill for this opportunity."

Smith did the math in his head: Britnee and the kids could split his assets and his insurance and be just fine. Worst-case scenario, if indictments came down after his death, they'd still have a ton of money. His ex-wives could fight over the scraps.

And he would get all the rest. With none of the bitching.

"In or out?"

He nodded at Diamond, with the decisive boldness that had made his name—his real name—synonymous with success. "In."

"Perfect," said Diamond. He pulled from his briefcase a stack of paperwork the size of a 19th-century Russian novel. "This may take a while."

◈

It took over four hours, according to Smith's Breitling Chronomat watch. They were now in what Diamond called the Eulogy Phase. The paperwork was signed, the $30 million was then transferred from one account to another to another until it finally made its way to Death, Inc. Plastic surgery was scheduled for the day after tomorrow. He was on his way to officially becoming Patrick Smith. At least they hadn't named him John.

"The most important thing," Diamond said, "is how we want you to die."

"I'd say heroically, but no one would believe that." He could step in front of an assassin's bullet and his enemies would accuse him of trying to upstage the President.

Diamond thumbed through the stack of papers. "Says here you like extreme sports. Bit of a thrill seeker, are you, Smith?"

"In life and in business."

"I think a sporting accident might be just the thing." Diamond looked up. "I assume you know how to sky-dive?"

"Of course."

"Good. That's our most popular death." Diamond opened his laptop. "We'll be responsible for the press release announcing your untimely demise. No one will know it came from us. Our connections run deep. Trust me, Smith."

"I'm impressed."

"You should be." Diamond's fingers hovered over the keypad. "Well?"

"What?"

"What would you like your eulogy to say?"

"Let's see." Smith stood and paced the office, as he liked to do when orating. "Of course, lead with how I'm a great businessman."

"Was."

"Was? Was!" Smith grinned. He could get to like this being dead stuff. "Squelch those embezzlement rumors. Proclaim my innocence!" He stopped pacing. What else was important to leave as his lasting impression upon the world? What should people think of when remembering him? "And oh, ya know, how I was a loving husband, good father, blah blah blah."

"All the usuals. Trust me, Smith. The world will hear of your death and be humbled. Even your enemies will weep. This isn't my first eulogy."

"I'll bet not." Smith leaned across the desk and spoke in a low, confidential tone. "So, were you a client?"

"Mr. Smith."

"Hey! What about Elvis?

"I'm warning you, Smith."

"Because I never thought he was *really* dead."

Diamond pursed his lips and looked at Smith with cat eyes more narrow than usual.

"You can tell me."

"Mr. Smith," Diamond said, "I am here to help you die. Don't make me have to kill you."

❖

Two hours later the Cessna 182 was circling the mountains. Smith had assumed he'd get a last night with Britnee, a chance for at least one final tussle. But, no—as soon as he'd signed off on his eulogy, Diamond had whisked him right into a waiting limo.

"So, what's the actual plan here?" said Smith.

Diamond helped him put on his parachute. "No need to worry." He motioned Smith to the open bay, leaned in close, and shouted over the *frap-frap-frap* of the engine. "Trust me."

"I just gave you 30 million dollars," Smith said. "If that's not trust—"

Diamond interrupted by shoving him out of the plane.

Smith cannonballed through the sky, clawing at the air like a cat at a scratching post, screaming with a pitch and power that Callas from the stage at La Scala couldn't best. He felt a rush of adrenalin, like hearing the opening bell of the stock market, and his survival instincts kicked in. Smith began to count. They'd been flying at 10,000 feet and he'd been falling for probably ten seconds, so: eleven, twelve... When Smith hit thirty seconds, he pulled the ripcord.

Which promptly came off in his hand.

But before he could sing his next aria, he was suddenly grabbed around the waist from behind. As he was jerked upward by the opening of a parachute and then began to slowly descend, he heard Diamond in his earpiece: "The scream was a nice touch, Smith. Good authenticity. The pilot will remember it when he reports your death."

That was when Smith wet himself and mercifully passed out.

❖

The next two weeks were a blur of surgeries and recoveries, drifting in and out of consciousness, and constant paperwork containing all the facts of the life of Patrick Smith. He had no idea where he was. The sharp sunlight through closed blinds suggested desert country.

His disappearance and probable death were all over CNN. And once they found his "unrecognizable" body the reportage intensified. One of his idols, a captain of industry, read Diamond's eulogy at his funeral. Poor Britnee must have been overcome with grief, clinging as she did to the arm of an attractive young man Smith didn't recognize. He took notice of the red-soled stilettos she wore to his funeral. But he wasn't angry: didn't she deserve new Louboutins at such a tragic time? His kids had the same sullen expressions they always wore, so. . . maybe they were sad? Meanwhile, his three ex-wives jockeyed for media attention.

In other words, life after death went on as usual.

It was all worth it, though, because his new face was amazing! Youthful, with only a whispered rumor of the unnatural. Nothing like the fake sheen of a Diamond. His nose was bolder, lips fuller, his tight chin and jawline proclaimed confidence. They'd tightened up his eyes a skosh, nothing too catlike, and traded his contacts for eyeglasses. But the magnification only made his eyes bluer, more piercing. He was so good-looking he could've turned himself gay. They'd even given his body some nips and tucks; tighter pecs, and the slight pooch of his belly was gone. Smith couldn't swear it, but he was pretty sure his aging testicles had been raised an inch.

Finally, the day to begin his new life was here. Smith showered (yes, definitely new balls), and was dressed and ready to go with an hour to spare.

Diamond dropped by. He extended a hand and whispered, "Mr. Smith, I presume?" They shared a conspiratorial laugh. Diamond settled Smith into a wheelchair for his dramatic exit.

"Ready?"

"Oh, yes."

"Good," said Diamond. From behind, he pulled a hypodermic from his jacket and aimed it at Smith's newly taut neck. "Trust me, Smith."

◈

A strange, rhythmic thump woke Mr. Patrick Smith. In his dream, a window shutter was banging during a rainstorm. Smith inhaled with a start and blinked. Even with his eyeglasses, it took a moment to get his bearings through the drug fog.

He was in a dark, dumpy room, crinked over in a sticky vinyl chair. The noise came from an oscillating fan knocking against a Formica-topped table. The fading wallpaper was coming loose at the seams, the floor was uncarpeted.

Smith rose with a wobble and turned the fan off. The air was instantly heavy, with a tangy sub-odor he placed as mold. The house was so small he could take it all in by merely turning his head. A living room with a kitchenette on one side and a closed door on the other, behind which a toilet ran unceasingly. The twin bed against the wall to his right seemed to indicate there was no separate bedroom. What was this place?

His confusion kept him from noticing at first the note stuck to the mini-fridge. As he yanked it out from under a magnet, his mouth went dry. He opened the refrigerator door. Milk, Velveeta cheese, PBR, store-brand ketchup. The cupboards offered boxed mac & cheese, packets of ramen, and canned soups. Smith cracked open a beer and downed half of it before he could bring himself to read the note.

"*Mr. Smith,*" it read. "*Welcome to Pacoima! We hope you enjoy your new home here at The Palm Grove Trailer Park. We've stocked you up with everything you'll need to get started. There's a payphone just across the parking lot until you get your own installed. Your car is the Dodge Dart in space E4. It's having some transmission problems, but nothing you can't get repaired. Keys are by the front door. Now, before you start worrying about how to pay for all this, you'll be happy to know we've opened a checking account for you, and deposited over $500! Strangely, your quarter-billion seems to have gone missing. Sorry about that, we can't imagine what happened! But to offset the loss, we've managed to procure honest employment for you. Congratulations, you're the new swing shift cashier at the Granny Burger on Delmont Avenue! It's two blocks east of here. You can't miss it. Most popular fast-food chain in the country, as you may have heard. You start tomorrow at 3:00 PM, so don't be late! It's been a pleasure working with you, Mr. Smith. Enjoy your new life!*"

Smith pulled a Kleenex from the box and wiped his runny eyes; must be the hot, dusty air. He drained his beer and contemplated having another. *Why not?* According to the Timex on his wrist, he didn't have to be at work for another 26 hours.

He cracked the beer open and raised it to his new lips. This wasn't the end. He'd fought far worse battles.

Swing shift cashier. Why, he'd be *manager* in a month.

In two months, he thought, *I'll own the franchise, mark my words! You can't keep the King of Granny Burger down!*

He laughed—slightly manic, yes, but laughter nevertheless. A good sign: it meant he wasn't giving in to adversity.

Because, *this?* This was nothing!

He drained his beer and released a long, satisfying belch. He grabbed another. The world would hear from Patrick Smith soon enough; just for tonight, though, he'd get good and tanked.

Today the franchise, tomorrow the world—his rise back to the top would be fun!

And his vengeance would be even better.

Art Young, "Capitalism," *Life*, February 23, 1911

CONTRIBUTORS' BIOGRAPHIES

EDITORS

ROGER NOKES (Editor-in-Chief; Twitter: @McCaffery_write
) writes fiction under the pseudonym Stanton McCaffrey. His short stories have been featured in *Dark Yonder*, *Mystery Magazine*, *Guilty*, *Mystery Tribune*, *Vautrin*, *Shotgun Honey*, and more. He has published two novels: *Into the Ocean*; and *Neighborhood of Dead Ends*.

ALBERT TUCHER (Contributing Editor; Twitter: @AlbertTucher) is the creator of prostitute Diana Andrews, who has appeared in more than 100 hardboiled stories in venues including *The Best American Mystery Stories 2010*. Her first longer case, the novella *The Same Mistake Twice*, was published in 2013. In 2017 Albert Tucher launched a second series set on the Big Island of Hawaii, in which *Pele's Prerogative* is the latest entry. He is a past president of the Mystery Writers of America NY Chapter. He lives in New Jersey, and loves NJ Turnpike jokes.

JAY BUTKOWSKI (Managing Editor; Twitter: @jtbutkowski
) is a writer of fiction, an eater of tacos and an amateur pizzaiolo who lives in New Jersey. His stories have appeared in online and

print publications, including *Shotgun Honey*, *Yellow Mama*, *All Due Respect*, *Dark Yonder*, and *Vautrin*, among others. He is a founding editor at **Rock and a Hard Place Press**, an independent publisher chronicling "bad decisions and desperate people." He's also a father of twins, a newlywed husband, and a middling pancake chef.

PAUL J. GARTH (Associate Editor; Twitter: @PauljGarth) is an editor for **Rock and a Hard Place Press**. His short fiction has been published in *Thuglit*, *Tough*, *Needle: A Magazine of Noir*, *Plots with Guns*, *Crime Factory*, **Rock and a Hard Place Magazine**, and several other anthologies and web magazines. His novella, *The Low White Plain*, part of the "A Grifter's Song" series, was released in June 2022. He lives and writes in Nebraska, where he lives with his family.

R.D. SULLIVAN (Associate Editor; Twitter: @_TheRussian) is a writer of fiction, comedy, and letters to the editor. Her work can be found at *Fireside Fiction Magazine*, *Shotgun Honey*, and *Tough*, as well as in the *Killing Malmon* and *Murder-A-Go-Go's* anthologies. She now lives in North Carolina with her kiddo and mutts, and is an aspiring woodland hermit. You can track her down over at govneh.com

ROB D. SMITH (Associate Editor; Twitter: @RobSmith3) is a common man attempting to write uncommon fiction in Louisville, KY. His work has appeared in *Apex Magazine*, *Shotgun Honey*, *The Arcanist*, *Pyre Magazine*, *Thriller Magazine*, *Bristol Noir*, **Rock and a Hard Place Magazine**, *Tough*, *Vautrin*, and several other crime, horror, and speculative anthologies and online magazines. Find more about him at https://robdsmith.carrd.co/

CONTRIBUTING WRITERS

(In order of appearance of work)

C.W. BLACKWELL (Twitter: @CW_Blackwell) is an American author from the Central Coast of California. His recent short stories have appeared with *Reckon Review*, *Shotgun Honey*, *Tough Magazine*, **Rock and a Hard Place Magazine**, and *Mystery Magazine*. He is a 2021 Derringer award winner and 2022 finalist. His fiction novellas *Song of the Red Squire* and *Hard Mountain Clay* are available where books are sold.

SCOTT VON DOVIAK (Twitter: @vondoviak)'s twenty-year pop culture writing career includes three books, and stints as a film critic for the *Fort Worth Star-Telegram* and a television reviewer for *The Onion's AV Club*. His short stories have appeared in *Tough*, *Shotgun Honey*, and **Rock and a Hard Place**, among others. His debut novel *Charlesgate Confidential* was named one of the top ten crime novels of 2018 by the *Washington Post*. His follow-up *Lowdown Road* is now available from Hard Case Crime. He lives in Austin, Texas.

ESTHER MUBAWA (Twitter: @EMubawa) is the pen name for a Zimbabwe woman who lives in Cape Town. She writes about the lives of Zimbabwean women. She has published stories in several magazines, including *Faultline*, *Common House*, *The Hooghly Review*, *Guernica*, and *Pikers Press*. She hopes to soon have enough published stories to put together in a collection.

JAMES D.F. HANNAH (Twitter: @jamesdfhannah) is the Shamus Award-winning author of the Henry Malone series, including the novels *Because the Night* and *She Talks to Angels*. His short fiction has appeared in *Best American Mystery and Suspense 2022*, edited by

Steph Cha and Jess Walter; *Playing Games*, edited by Lawrence Block; ***Under the Thumb: Stories of Police Oppression***, edited by S.A. Cosby; *Vautrin*; *Shotgun Honey*; and *The Anthology of Appalachian Writers*. He lives in Louisville, Kentucky, where all the bourbon is.

AD SCHWEISS (Twitter: @ADSchweiss) is a trial lawyer who lives and works in Northern California.

THOMAS TRANG (Twitter: @heyThomasTrang) is a French/Vietnamese writer currently living in the UK after stints in New York and Singapore. His stories have previously appeared in *FutureQuake*, *Shotgun Honey*, and the *Revolutions 2* anthology. He is currently working on a SF trilogy which mixes cyberpunk with the gritty realpolitik of *The Wire*.

MEIRAV DEVASH (Twitter: @MeiravDevash) and **EDDIE McNAMARA** (Twitter: @EddieMcNamara) are writers living in New York City. They're currently working on a satanic panic horror novel together. They share a bank account and would both appreciate it if you bought a copy of Eddie's novel, *Brooklyn Hardcore*.

ANDREW RUCKER JONES is a former IT dweeb and American expatriate living in Germany with his Georgian wife and their three children. His greatest literary achievement to date is authoring ninety-eight iCloud reminders for every household chore from cleaning sinks to checking smoke detectors. Learn more at http://selfdefeatistnavelgazing.wordpress.com/

SAM WIEBE (Twitter: @sam_wiebe) is the author of the Wakeland novels, one of the most authentic and acclaimed detective series in Canada. He also writes (allegedly) as Nolan Chase. *A Lonesome Place for Dying* comes out May 2024 from Crooked Lane.

CURTIS IPPOLITO (Twitter: @curtis9980) is the author of the crime novel *Burying the Newspaper Man*. He is an Anthony Award Finalist (2023) and Derringer Award Finalist (2023). He is a member of Sisters in Crime and serves on the board of the San Diego SinC chapter. Learn more about him at curtisippolito.com

TIM P. WALKER (Twitter: @walkertimp) is currently celebrating the fact that the student loans he was paying for over half his life are no more. His work has appeared in such publications as **Rock and a Hard Place**, *Out of the Gutter*, and the late great *Baltimore City Paper*. He has also had his short fiction published in several anthologies, including **Under the Thumb: Stories of Police Oppression** and the 2023 Bouchercon anthology, *Killin' Time in San Diego*. He lives in Baltimore, Maryland.

JESSE LEE, who publishes novels and poetry under another name, is originally from the Golden State and since childhood has traveled widely. Currently Jesse writes noir and dances hip hop in New York City.

SEAN LOGAN's stories have appeared in more than forty publications, including *Black Static*, *Nightscript*, and the anthologies *American Gothic*, *Dark Visions*, and *Laughing at Shadows*. He lives in Northern California with his wife, their five-year-old twins, and a giant white Kuvasz that may be part polar bear.

TOM ANDES (Twitter: @thomaseandes)'s writing has appeared in *Best American Mystery Stories 2012*, *Santa Monica Review*, *Valparaiso Fiction Review*, and many other places. He won the 2019 Gold Medal for Best Novel-in-Progress from the Pirate's Alley Faulkner Society, a New Orleans-based literary organization. He works as a freelance editor, book coach, manuscript consultant, teaches, moonlights as a country singer, and released his debut EP, "Static on Every Station" on Bandcamp in 2022. He also plays guitar with Emily Neustrom and the Fried Honeys. He can be found at www.tomandes.com

STEVEN-ELLIOT ALTMAN is a bestselling science fiction author and award-winning videogame writer. He's been trusted with some diverse major brands; including Batman, Sherlock Holmes, Ancient Aliens and *The Wizard of Oz*. Steve penned and narrative-designed the Facebook sensation *Pearl's Peril*, which boasts 90+ million players! His recent game projects include *Ancient Aliens: The Game* and *Project Blue Book: Hidden Mysteries*, and his latest game is *Terminator: Dark Fate*, based on the feature film.

Steven's novels include *Captain America is Dead*, *Zen in the Art of Slaying Vampires*, *Batman: Fear Itself*, *The Killswitch Review*, *The Irregulars* and *Deprivers*. In reviews of note his writing has been compared to that of Stephen King, Dean Koontz, Michael Crichton, and Philip K. Dick, and he has collaborated with world class writers such as Neil Gaiman, Michael Reaves, Harry Turtledove and Dr. Janet Asimov. Steve's latest novel, *Severed Wings*, is available from WordFire Press.

LIN MORRIS lives and writes in his hometown of Portland, OR. His work has appeared in *Unlikely Stories*; *Trembling with Fear*; *Flumes Literary Journal*; *Little Old Lady Comedy*; *Meet Cute Press*; *Second Chance Lit*; *Suddenly and Without Warning*; and in the anthologies *Flash of Brilliance*, *Coffin Blossoms*, *Breathless*, *TWF v. 3*, and *Bullshit Lit*. His novels *Spot the Not* and *The Marriage Wars* are available on amazon.com. He won the 2020 YeahWrite Micro Fiction Competition. He is proudly left-handed and considers this to be his preeminent trait.